This Way and That

By the author

Young Adult Fiction

Grandad's Extraordinary Camper Van
Those Among Us
Those Among Us Return

The Scott Series

Ten Quests (Book one)
Ten Kingdoms (Book two)
Ten Keys (Book three)
Ten Trolls (Book four)

Anthology

This Way and That

This Way and That

by John Edward Parsons

2020

This Way and That

Cataloging information
ISBN: 978-1-999684-86-0

Acknowledgements

I must take this opportunity to thank my wife, Jennifer, who suffered the stress of my continual disappearance into my den while writing this book.
She really knows how lonely 'lock down' can be.
Jen has been ever patient with me and guided me to give you, the reader, what I hope will be success in the first short stories book I have had published.
Thank you, Jen, for your suggestions and the amount of checks you did for me on my grammar and spelling!
This is our baby Jen,
Thank you.

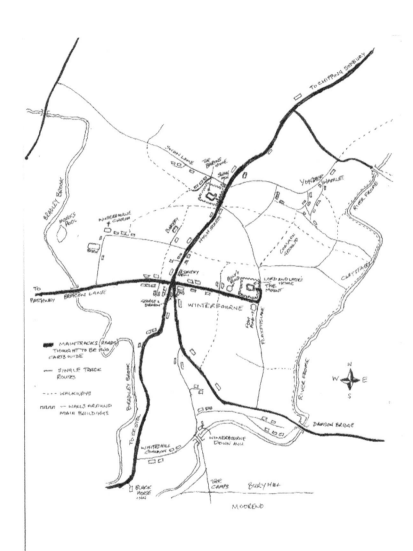

CONTENTS

The Story of Watley's End

I live in a village called Winterbourne and have done so for the last fifty odd years.

Some things in village life puzzle me, and until recently, the name of a hamlet near Winterbourne, got me intrigued.

I had not done any major research on it, but just by chance, I purchased an old map of the village and the surrounds.

Now it appears that the original name for the hamlet was 'Yonder'.

Yes, I know what you are thinking, I thought it strange also.

It seems that the scattering of houses outside of the village of Winterbourne had no name, so when locals were asked where they lived, they pointed and said Yonder.

This got me doing more research and I found the church had old written logs of the burning and purging of witches in the parish.

Wonderful words assailed me as I read about one witch in 1783, who was burned at the stake in the hamlet of Yonder.

It seems that she had been practicing medicine and had cured many. People came from far and wide to see her, and most times she was able to help if not cure them.

The Baron who held charge over the peasants in three villages, heard about this, and was not well pleased.

The people were supposed to be servile to

him, and only him. To have someone who had a little more than cow shit for brains, was unthinkable, and he now had one on his land.

What to do about it?

Declare she was a witch and the give her a trial, find her guilty and burn her.

Persecuting suspected witches was not an elite plot against the poor; nor was practicing witchcraft a mode of peasant resistance.

The church and state alike tried and executed them. It took more than pure reason to bring the witch to justice, she could incite the lower orders to think and it was best to remove the problem by letting the lower orders demand it through fear.

So it was that the Baron set about bringing doubt into the peasant's minds. A woman who went into her hut, was later found to have lost her child, the rumour started that she was well before she entered the witches hut.

A witch. At the utterance of the word, the people shuddered, wasn't it said that a witch is a friend of the devil?

They crossed themselves and looked around, and so as each misfortune occurred, so the witch was blamed.

Reason didn't come into the thinking behind this. A few weeks ago, she was a good friend, now people took to bathing in the river to clean the hand that may have touched them.

In so doing, they washed the filth from them, and felt better for it. They had been purged from the evil that had been upon them said the priest, and the church began to get offerings of cabbage and potatoes once again.

Weeks later, the Baron rode down to the hut and called the woman out.

Two soldiers held her, and she was charged with being a witch.

"You will get a fair trial, and then we will burn you at the stake," he said.

She had her hands tied and a rope put about her neck, then with the Baron on his horse and the two soldiers behind him, he led her away from her hut, as she stumbled behind the soldier's horses.

At his manor house, she was locked in a small stock room and then left for the trial the next day.

On the following morning, the Baron, having had a hearty breakfast, ordered the woman to be brought out before him.

The local priest was commanded to write the proceedings down. A chair was brought out for the Baron to sit in judgement over her trial.

People had come to be a witness, and the peasants were told to attend. Not to see justice done, but to endorse the idea that he could always be relied upon to look after their welfare.

The woman, who had had no food of water since her arrest, looked a mess.

She was made to kneel before her superior and not to look at him.

He told the people that she could cast a spell upon him just by looking at him.

Everyone made the sign of the cross, and the Baron smiled. The woman had been judged already.

He then asked who among those here accuse this woman of witchcraft.

A woman pushed through the people and said, "I do."

She was bent and frail, her face distorted and wrinkled and etched with grime.

No one had seen her before.

This was hardly surprising, as the Baron had found her a long way away and told her what to say. He promised to pay her well to accuse the woman of witchcraft.

"How may you charge this woman that you accuse of being a witch?" asked the Baron.

"I was young when I went into her lair, but she stole my youth, and now I am as she was."

There was fear now within the people who again crossed themselves and vowed to wash the stench she was giving out from their bodies, lest they catch something evil.

"How say thee witch, will you reverse your spell and give this creature who lives in your old body, her own back?"

The woman lifted her head and as she looked around, the people shut their eyes so that she could not see into their souls.

"I do not know this woman. She means nothing to me," the accused woman uttered.

"Then by your own mouth, you have confirmed your fate. I find you guilty of witchcraft and condemn you to be burnt at the stake." He turned to the people, "What say you god fearing men and women?"

To shouts of "Burn her," and "Guilty," the

woman was hauled away to wait for her final day.

She was given bread and water; it was much better to burn a live witch than a dead one.

In two days, a cross was made and stood tall in a field outside of the hamlet of Yonder.

On the third day after the trial, the woman was dragged out and put in a cart.

She was paraded through the three villages and soon a gathering of people followed the Baron sat on his horse, who was leading the cart to the burning site.

Once they arrived, the two soldiers tied rope around her wrists, and threw the rope over the cross bars.

Passing the ropes end to two men, they waited as the priest said his prayer, asking god to shut the door of forgiveness for the likes of she who did the devils bidding.

Once he finished, Baron Watley said, "Three men to each rope, pull her up."

Hands grabbed the rope, and, in a few moments, the woman was hoisted up to the cross beams.

A ladder was taken from the cart and a soldier climbed up to one cross beam and tied a new rope tight around her hand and arm. He called for the main rope to be released and he untied it and it fell to the ground.

He then repeated the procedure on the other side.

Another cart came with hay stubble, sticks and logs.

Soon the pyre was ready.

The Baron got down from his horse and asked for someone to strike some flint, that he may light the fire and send this witch back from whence she came from.

Soon a small stick with straw and hay tied to it was lit and the torch was passed to the Baron.

He walked to the pyre and lit the straw and soon it was burning well. They threw on more sticks to make sure the fire took, and as he turned to walk away, so the witch called out to him.

"Ye who hath condemned me falsely, shall on the seventh day from my death, join me in purgatory for ever more."

The Baron turned and as he looked up to her, she smiled, and he felt a cold shiver run down his spine.

She writhed as she burnt, but not a sound came from her lips, and those watching crossed their hearts in fear that she was not dying but changing into a devil.

They watched her head slump forward, and soon the fire overwhelmed her. They moved back as the smell of burning flesh came to them, then started to drift away as everything tumbled into the flames.

Soon there was truly little of the frame to see, and the body had been lost to the flames when everything fell.

"You lad," said the Baron, "stay here and see that the fire doesn't spread anywhere. When the flame dies, then you can return home."

The Baron got onto his horse and with his two soldiers, returned to his manor.

He took his usual mug of ale and thought of the way the woman had died.

Had she really been a witch?

The heat had been intense, he had to move back himself as it built up. But to burn like that and to not even scream, could she have put a curse upon him?

He slept badly that night and on the following morning, rose and had a good breakfast.

He had just finished his meal when a servant came to him.

He was told that a man wanted to speak to him and to ask a boon of him.

"Tell him to wait," he said, and walked to a window that looked toward the place of the burning.

As he looked, he could just make out a spiral of smoke rising up from the area he estimated that the burning had occurred.

He turned and shouted to the servant, "Saddle my horse and call out my guards, there's mischief afoot."

Going down the stairs he saw the man who had requested an audience with him.

"Well man, tell me quickly what you want. You can see I am busy and have need to be on my way within a few moments."

"Sir, my son who you told last evening to watch over the dying embers of the burning, has not come home all night. I did go to the ashes, but they still burn, and they burn with much heat. He did not return home for you told him to stay until the flame dies, and it has not done so."

"Upon my soul man. If this is because that wretch of yours has been casting wood to the fire, then I shall have him, and you flogged for your impertinence."

"Sir, no wood has gone onto the ashes, but when I approached the fire, it rose, then fell again. It is as if the devil himself," and he crossed himself, "is under the ashes. It is fearsome hot Sir."

The Baron mounted his horse and with the two soldiers, he rode out from his manor and towards the rising plume of smoke.

The man ran after them but was soon left behind.

Upon arrival to the place, he was surprized to see many of the people who had attended the burning, standing around the ashes that truly had a flame coming from the middle of the pile of ash.

"Boy, where is the boy who I told to watch over the flames from the burning, where are you boy?"

The boy who had been asked to stay ran up to the Baron.

"Have you been throwing kindling onto this boy?"

"No Sir, but as someone moves towards the pile of ash, so the flame grows higher."

The Baron got down from his horse and said to one of the soldiers, "Hold the boy. If I find a lie has been told to me, I will push a branch of wood up his arse, and he will join the witch's ashes."

The Baron walked toward the smoking ashes and suddenly a flame came from the centre of the pile and as he drew closer, so it also grew.

He stopped and then moved around the pile, looking for any sign of any new wood, but saw none.

As he completed his circle, so the boy's father arrived.

"Release the boy, he tells the truth," said the Baron.

He turned to the crowd and said. "Get water from the river, we shall dowse this fire and end this foolery."

The people went away and all, but a few remained.

Still the flame burned.

A while later, a cart came with a barrel of water and buckets.

Water was poured from the barrel into a bucket and a man approached the flame.

"Get on with it man," said the Baron as he watched the man.

He threw the water towards the flame but although some went on it, most fell short.

"Give me a bucket, I will show you how to deal with this."

A bucket was passed to the Baron and he walked quickly towards the flame and threw the lot directly onto it.

Great clouds of steam flew upwards and ash also blew upwards with the steam, but still the flame burned.

"Another, give me another."

Another bucket was passed to him and again

he threw it over the flame. Again, a large amount of steam rose from the ashes and as it spat, so the ashes rose up with the steam.

Then the screaming started among the people standing around the flame, that still had not died down.

Baron Watley turned to see what was going on, and hot water vapour burnt his face and hands. As he shouted out in pain, he breathed in some of the hot steam and some of the fine ash in the vapour.

His face was burning with the hot steam and ash clung to his face.

He struggled to walk to his horse, but the water and ash hindered his efforts. He broke out from the area, and as he lifted his tunic to wipe his face, the people and his two guards turned and ran away.

The baron heard a noise above him and looked up.

The vapour was now in the shape of a female and as he watched, one of her hands reached down and went into his opened mouth.

He heard laughing as he gagged at the taste of the ash.

And then it all ended.

The steam dropped to the ground, the dust blew away, and the flame died down and vanished.

The Baron mounted his horse and rode away from the fire, and towards the people and his guards who were standing watching him come to them.

"The fire is out, no thanks to any of you. You

two, go and get your mounts, I need to clean this filth from my clothes and my body. Then a good jug of ale and I will then give thought to your punishment."

He rode through the crowd who parted for him and made his way to his manor.

He stripped his tunic and his trousers and commanded that they be scrubbed clean, then asked for water that he could rinse the ash from his face and hands.

Once clean, he sat in his chair and called for ale.

He drank well and soon felt tired.

When he woke the next day, he was aware that he felt uncomfortable in his stomach. Had the ale been off? He thought not.

As the evening wore on, his pain grew even more.

He called for his physician and begged for a potion to take the pain in his stomach away.

After an examination of him, the physician suggested it was wind, and pressed his enlarged stomach.

The Baron let out a thunderous fart, but it smelt of burning flesh.

Holding his nose, the medic said, "Having eased the blockage of air within you Sir, I am sure you will be a lot more comfortable," and he made a quick exit.

The Baron went to sleep but the following day, all was not well.

His face and hands had blisters where the steam had burnt him as he threw the water over the fire.

The physician was again called but on seeing the large blisters, suggested that he bleed him to purify his blood, for that is what it must be.

He took out a large leech and tried to get it to fasten on the Barons arm, but as the bloodsucker bit in, so it died.

After six attempts, the man decided that enough leeches had died, it was time to lance the blisters.

Four men were called to hold the Baron down and once held; the physician cut the first blister.

Pus oozed out and again the smell of burning flesh attacked their nostrils.

The Baron smelt nothing; he couldn't understand how four grown men could be so affected by the bursting of a blister. The pain from doing it was his not theirs.

The physician continued with the lancing, and with each cut, the ooze gave forth more odious smells of burnt flesh and blood.

Finally, the lancing was finished, and the physician left the Baron, but he continued to feel ill, and food nor ale interested him anymore.

He became exhausted and slept for longer periods. Day or night became as nothing to him.

He woke on another day with his tongue swollen, blisters and puss seeping from them as they broke.

His time awake was plagued with pain.

On the seventh day, the Baron failed to rise from his bed.

Servants didn't know what to do, but then

his valet said he would go to the bedroom and wake the Baron.

He found the Baron dead.

Again, the smell of burnt flesh was evident in the room.

As word spread of the demise of Baron Watley, so the curse from the woman also was also told and linked to his death.

People feared the demons who must be now be roaming in the hamlet of Yonder.

Slowly, the people left their huts and moved away, always looking back yonder at the place of Watley's end.

The hamlet became known as Watley's end, and as time moved on, so the story died, until I found it.

Now the old hamlet of Yonder, known as Watley's end, is part of Winterbourne. But if you should walk down Watley's end road, you will come to the end with a field in front of you. Court road then starts.

This is where I think, the Baron held court over the woman he burnt as a witch. The field was the site of the burning, convenient for the three villages of Frampton Cotterell, The Heath, (now known as Coalpit Heath) and Winterbourne to see the burning of a witch.

It is said by those who live nearby, that on some nights, the wind sounds as if the woman still screams at the injustice laid upon her.

And that's the answer to why the name of Watley's End is to be found in Winterbourne in South Gloucestershire.

Author's Note

This story is completely made up. Some people have asked me why I have not put the references to the books I took notes from.
The references are all from my head.
I even drew a map of 'Old Winterbourne' to help me write and describe the characters in my stories walking the paths through the village and surrounds.

JP

The Two of Them

I had seen them before standing there. In fact, I see them at this time every year.

No matter what the weather, they come and stand there, silent, and still.

You may wonder why I am telling you this.

Well, truth to tell, I wonder myself.

You see, I know why I see them each year, and it's quite a story of love.

I think I will begin by going back to the start, always the best place to go for a story.

They had both been born within a few days of each other.

Neither mother had had an easy time of giving birth, but then what woman does?

The mothers were in the same ward as each other, and a bond had formed between them both.

They found that they lived a few streets away from each other, and it seemed natural to continue meeting once they left the hospital.

The pleasing thing was that both husbands also got on well with each other, and the bond became closer still.

The mothers would walk together whenever possible, and if one baby was ill, then the other would offer support.

The children grew, as baby's do, both healthy and strong.

They would play together and shared in an almost knowing way.

Mary Jane was a pretty child and as she grew, so her features enhanced what I perceived was going to help her to become a real beauty.

Josh was a good-looking baby, but again, development enhanced his looks and his growth.

They both went to pre-school together, and then to the 'real' school as they were told.

They were never short of friends, and although they played with others, they always managed to be near each other.

They moved into junior school, and the pair were now becoming two fine looking youngsters.

Mary Jane was stunning even at that young age, yet never failed to give and support her friends around her. She would often cuddle a girl that had fallen over, talking softly to her.

Everyone felt she was part of their being. She never forced her way or her opinion on anyone, but somehow seemed to be the guide in organising play.

Josh was always near. He joined in sports with his friends and was always the 'gentleman' when playing the game.

Both worked through the junior school, always growing, and becoming better at all they did.

Learning seemed no problem to either one.

They helped their struggling friends to solve things that gave them problems and never ridiculed any for their lack of understanding.

Together they moved up to the senior school,

and both were placed in the same classroom on the first day of school.

Both were selected for streaming; such were their capabilities.

Again, they made new friends, and maintained their old ones.

Josh had started to fill out, his shoulders broadened, and his looks were something that the girls seemed to pick up on.

Mary Jane had started to turn into a young woman, with her shape changing and her still radiant good looks making the boys in the higher classes turn their heads.

Some approached her, and asked for a date, but she declined.

They worked through the school years, and on school holiday's, went for walks together, talking of music, shows and things that interested them.

When one went away for a holiday, they messaged each other.

They became a pair without realising it.

Realisation came when out walking through the park, and talking about future aspirations, their hands moved together, and for the first time they touched.

The way it was explained was, it just happened, and when it did, it was like an electric shock. They stopped walking, looked at each other's hands still holding, then smiled and continued walking.

Mary Jane and Josh had progressed through the different years, always in the same class. At the end of each key stage year, they sat in various examinations and their academic achievement was evaluated against the national curriculum levels.

Both ended with extraordinary high-level achievements.

Coming up to the final year they sat A level exams for qualifications to go to university.

Josh was aiming at becoming a doctor, Mary Jane wanted to explore the many areas of the sciences.

They came away with straight 'A's.

They both set about writing applications to universities and were aware that they would not be near each other for a long time.

As they waited to hear if they were to be accepted, they worked in a cafe, serving customers, and clearing and cleaning tables.

Eventually, the offers came.

Josh had applied to Oxford and Bristol, both offered him a place.

Mary Jane had applied to the University of Cambridge, and its School of Biological Sciences. She was offered a place.

Josh accepted Oxford; Mary Jane accepted to go to Cambridge.

When it came to the time to go their own ways, it made them feel that a part of them was being ripped in two.

In all the time that they had been in their relationship, no sex had occurred.

True, there had been the touching, but both had agreed both verbally and by silent consent, that the final act would wait.

They kissed each other goodbye, both strong

in their conviction that there would be no other.

They had talked about the social side, and yes, they both knew that there would be liaisons, but that this would go nowhere to spoil their love for each other.

And love each other they did.

Including the foundation year, Mary Janes course would be four years.

Josh for his course would be four years which if he passed the exam, would then entail a further three years, after this, if his qualifications were high enough, he could do further studies to become a specialist on a particular field of medicine.

The day came when they left each other.

She cried, he cried. Each wiped their tears away, looked at each other and tears fell once again. It was a hard and sad parting.

"You are mine," said Josh.

"And you are mine," said Mary Jane.

University days went quicker than they each expected. They both enjoyed the courses and found good friends who they joined on a few nights out to parties or dancing in clubs.

Mary Jane had one or two young men try to persuade her to join him in his bed, but this was firmly rebuffed.

She gained the nickname of the 'iced maiden.' She knew about this, her friends said why not, but she always said "No."

Josh was sought out by the females, some openly suggested that he examined her in the deepest way, but he refused.

He danced with many, but never joined the

many who went to the less wholesome places, here sex and drugs were available.

At times when the academic term ended, he and Mary Jane would return home and meet again.

They renewed their promise to each other with soft caresses and long lingering kisses, but the final step did not come.

Oh, they wanted to, desperate to, but they both helped each other, and they stayed firm in that promise to each other.

The years slipped by and still the pair resisted all who tried to share part of their lives.

On one occasion when Josh was examining a young woman with his consultant watching on, one female suggested that she had two bumps he could examine, and maybe cure another itch she had.

Josh ignored her and gave his pronouncement as to what he felt was the problem with the patient.

His Consultant was incredibly pleased then asked the female who had whispered to Josh, what would she suggest was the best course of action.

She hesitated then made her reply.

She was told to wait after the ward round, and he would have a word with her.

Later Josh heard that the consultant was particularly good at lip reading!

The years passed and, on every occasion, they met and expressed their love for each other. Still the final act was not done.

And five years came and went. Both were

exhausted, both had done exceptionally well, but now before the completion of their studies, they wanted time together.

They talked about going away together, to have special time with each other.

Both confessed that they wanted to make the final step, but something held them back.

They spoke to their parents, who were delighted that they were still an item.

"Josh has three more years of studying to do, and I have been offered a chance to join a research company for a year."

"We want to get married and would like both of our families blessing."

Both were extremely happy with the news and arrangements started to form for a wedding.

The usual questions were quietly asked, "Are you pregnant?"

The answer gave both families a lot of joy.

So, the plans were made, Josh went back to university for his three-year course, Mary Jane started her year with her company doing research.

Both of their parents joined in to put a deposit down for a two-bedroom cottage that the children had wanted.

It was a chocolate box looking place, in bad repair, but they all mucked in and over the six months, it was brought into shape.

They loved it.

By the end of the year, when Josh returned, they had everything arranged.

The day came and the wedding was perfect.

Mary Jane glowed as she walked down the aisle, and Josh, with a grin as wide as could be, watched his wife to be, come towards him.

With the final words. "I now pronounce you man and wife," they at last became a married couple.

After the celebrations, they slipped away and arrived at their cottage.

She unlocked the door, and he picked her up and carried her over the threshold.

He kicked the door closed and as he carried her upstairs to the bedroom, they kissed with passion, knowing that all they had waited for, would be fulfilled this night.

He was gentle with her, but both had an urgency and that night, their love had no boundaries.

On the following Monday, Josh left his bride and went back to the university, and Mary Jane returned to her job working in a laboratory.

I saw her quite a lot in those periods of loneliness, but Josh phoned her often, and returned home on some weekends.

When Josh returned home at a term break, Mary Jane told him that she was pregnant.

They were overjoyed with the news, and so were their parents who had been wanting for this news for a long time.

Josh had to return for the next course and Mary Jane went back to work, knowing that their parents were there if she wanted them.

At six months into her pregnancy, she had a problem, and her father-in-law drove her to the hospital.

She had a check-up and they did a few scans to see what was going on.

They told her that she had a major problem in carrying the baby, and the bleeding was the first sign.

She and all the family were horrified to hear this. Mary Jane begged them not to worry Josh. She would be okay.

As she went on into her pregnancy, she needed more care, but still she said nothing to Josh.

At seven months she was taken into hospital and they said that they needed to do a small operation on her.

She stayed in for three days, and Josh, who had been told that all was not well, came home and went to her bedside.

Mary Jane had lost a lot of weight and looked nothing like her old self.

The glow in her eyes was gone, she seemed to be in constant pain and Josh begged her to try to find out what was going on.

She looked at him and said, "Josh, our baby is important to us both. It will be our child, the symbol of our love, but my darling, I may not be here to put him or her to my breast."

Josh had tears in his eyes when he asked why and what was going on.

"I have cancer, they are holding it back, but not winning."

Josh took her into his arms and they both cried together.

Eventually, he asked, "Would an operation to remove it save you?"

"That was my question Josh, but I would suffer the loss of our baby, and even then, not live long after the operation."

Josh felt that there must be something that could be done, but knew that the deadly truth was, Mary Jane was going to leave him.

He never returned to the university, they understood of course.

Josh was by her side as long as he could.

The doctors were aware that he was studying to be a doctor and kept him appraised of every stage.

Before the full term, Mary Jane went into a trauma, she was losing blood and the medical team all rushed to her.

She was shaking and sweating, but even then, she had the sense to reach out to hold Josh's hand as she looked at him and gave him her last smile.

They pushed Josh away, he was reluctant to let go of her hand, but he allowed them to take him to a side room and sit down.

Sometime later, a doctor came to him and said, "We have saved your son, he is a fine healthy boy, but he will need to go into the premature baby unit to build him up. Once he is at a sound weight and we are happy with him, you will be able to take him home. It is no consolation, but your wife knew that she would not come through this. She was a very brave lady. I am sorry we could not do more."

Josh was allowed to see his son, and to sit with Mary Jane.

He touched her face, kissed her lips, and told

her he loved her, and always would.

Along with many others I attended the funeral of Mary Jane in Winterbourne church.

I held Josh for a brief moment, before moving on, tears were in my eyes also, we could say nothing to each other.

Three months later, Josh brought Mark home.

The parents helped, and after a long period, Josh returned to finish his medical degree.

He wasn't the man I had seen when they got married.

The light had gone from within him, yet when he returned and held Mark, I could almost see a small glow come back into his eyes as he gently rocked his son.

The first year came and on the date that she died, he took Mark to the crematorium where a plaque that had Mary Janes ashes beneath it was. The wording said, 'A mother for a moment, a heart ache for a lifetime.'

They stood for a while talking to her.

His Mother and Father and her parents all came together, to join the homage to a brave daughter, wife, and mother.

And that brings me back to today.

There stands a man who lost his wife, and a son who never knew his Mother.

Josh's parents are no longer with him. A tragic car accident took them from him, a year after his wife died.

And who am I?

Well, my wife died three years after our daughter died. She never recovered from the loss.

I am the father of Mary Jane, and I always come on this day, as I have for the last eight years.

Authors note

This story was inspired by a gravestone in Winterbourne churchyard.
It is a most interesting and poignant gravestone epitaph and is on the "Maids Grave," situated behind the church in line with the West Wall.
It is dedicated to Hannah, wife of Robert Fouracre, who died in 1829, and is a sad reflection of that time.

"Thirty years I was a maid
thirteen months a wife
four hours I was a mother and then I lost my life,
Behold my friend and cast an eye
then go thy way prepare to die
repent with speed make no delay
in my prime was called away."

A Sign of our Times

It had been four months now since Sebastian had helped her move into her new home.

Millicent looked around and thought how she had now become accustomed to living in this small house. Her original house she was forced to leave, would have used this as a broom cupboard.

She moved to her favourite chair, rubbing her hand along the headrest as she came around it to sit down.

Her son, Sebastian had arranged the move and the finances for the purchase of the house.

He is a good son really, she thought as she lowered herself into the chair.

Millicent's husband inconveniently died and left her with debts and a home mortgaged to the bank.

He had wasted the money on useless investments and his mistress, who had made sure she got well and truly looked after, in more than one way it would seem.

As her son had been sorting out the mess, the truth had shocked her.

She had said to him, "My god at his age and with someone so young. Don't men ever stop wanting to do that sort of thing? I hold her responsible for his death, too much excitement can do that to a man of his mature years."

Sebastian had said something like, "Mother, I am amazed that he had a mistress. I just hope I inherit his stamina."

It soon became clear that she would need to let the big house go to the bank and she would need to find somewhere to live.

She had to leave her closeted life, dismiss all her servants, and live among those who served her.

The ignominy of it was endorsed when her so called friends cut her dead. They had no time for those who could not maintain their social standing. They made all sorts of excuses to stop her coming to their homes for the usual game of bridge. She did so love the game, and the juicy gossip about everyone.

Now she was the subject of the gossip.

This was why she moved from London, and into this cupboard in Cheltenham.

Her sister lived nearby, but so far; Millicent had not contacted her. She meant to do this, but it was a long time since they spoke, and time had distanced them both.

She had been aware that her younger sister had been married three times, and that she was not short of money. All of her husbands had left a large amount to her, and it had been said that her last husband had died with a smile on his face.

I wonder if Clarence did also.

Her thoughts returned to Sebastian. His father and she had picked out a suitable woman, of particularly good breeding to marry.

But much to her annoyance, he had told her that he would pick his own woman. The prestige of the family name would be lost if he followed the statements that described <u>young people</u> of today as being "among the brave and the bold" who want to "be adventurous and out and about."

If adventurous was what she thought it meant, then Sebastian would definitely not be taking any care.

It's a mad world I am now living in, she thought.

And now we have this Chinese thing. Coronavirus 19.

I must have missed the other 18, while I was travelling the world with Clarence. As an ambassadors wife, one tends to miss these inconveniences, she thought.

She picked up the remote and put the television on.

The Secretary of State for Health and Social Care, Matt Hancock was speaking about the young people having impromptu party gatherings.

"The old slogan, 'Stay safe, stay in, and wash your hands,' had gone by the board now, Matt," she said to the television.

Now the new slogan is 'Look after Granny.'

Millicent a Granny? Fortunately, Sebastian had not yet told her that he had got any woman pregnant.

She listened for a short while longer.

"Well this non-Granny must look after herself," she said to Matt Hancock as she turned the programme off.

She had been in lockdown for quite a while now. It sounded like a jail sentence.

"Well this won't do," she said as she rose from her chair.

It was her day to go shopping and it was quite a walk.

Betty, one of her new friends, had offered to pick her up and take her to the supermarket, as she had been doing for a few weeks now.

This arrangement was under this 'bubble' practise. Such a stupid term in Millicent's opinion.

It made it sound as if Betty and she were going out for a smoke in some hookah bar.

Millicent put on her coat and pushed her purse into the pocket.

As Betty pulled up, Millicent locked the door and walked up to the gate with her umbrella just in case.

Betty jumped out and opened the back door.

"Better put your mask on Millicent, we don't want any problems, do we?"

Millicent pulled it from her pocket and before she put it on said, "I think the supermarket entrance should have had a giant mask over the front entrance. We could then go through the mask knowing they were robbers going to fleece us. It is scandalous how the prices have gone up since this virus came."

Betty laughed; she was quite used to Millicent's ways.

It was not long driving to the store, and once there, they set about getting the wheeled basket as they entered.

With their masks on, and they waited their turn, social distancing outside being observed.

Soon it came to their chance to enter.

Millicent had her umbrella in the basket, and she had rubbed the handle down with the disinfectant she had brought with her.

"There is no need to bring your own disinfectant madam," said a young girl as she entered.

"Young lady, if I touch your dispenser that has been handled by hundreds of people I know nothing about, can you guarantee that I will not catch something nasty that they have left on it for me?"

"But you would wipe your hands and then kill any germs madam."

"Then I have saved a few million unwanted bacteria for the next person to enjoy, haven't I? I will remain safe with my own precautions thank you."

So, saying, Millicent entered the aisle and made her way staying behind Betty.

She stopped at the packed vegetables and selected some tomatoes, and some carrots.

As she went to move on, a man passed her, stopping just in front of her, and started picking packs to go in his trolly.

Millicent took in a deep breath, put on her best affronted face and narrowing her eyes, said, "Young man, you clearly have no concept of social distancing. You have just invaded my space,"

The man slowly stood up straight from bending towards the shelves.

"Are you talking to me missis?"

Millicent looked around, then back at the

man.

"I see no other ignorant person in my space, do you?"

"Well, bleedin move back then, and it will be my space. And don't call me ignorant, I might not be a posh old git like you, but I'm educated the same as you and don't forget it."

"I very much doubt that," said Millicent as she held her umbrella out to stop someone else passing her.

The man glared at her and moved on muttering about 'old cows'.

Millicent turned to the backlog of customers and said, "I am sorry for the delay, once I have finished here, you will be able to move into this space."

The manager came through the crowd of shoppers and asked what was going on.

"Don't stand near me, you are in my space. How dare you infect my area," she said brandishing her umbrella.

"Madam, you need to keep moving, that's how it works. People can overtake and still maintain the desired social distancing. Now if you turn and face the shelves, I will direct those behind you to pass you safely."

He stepped away from her slightly and told people to overtake, and Millicent turned her head away as they passed.

"May I ask who you are? You are certainly protecting Granny as Matt Hancock said to me earlier on."

The man gaped at Millicent for a short while then said, "My name is Paul Grinton, I am the manager here. Did I hear correctly that you spoke earlier to the Secretary of State for Health and Social Care, Matt Hancock?"

"You correctly heard what I said young man. I speak to him now and again. For him to say that I am a granny is stupid, my son hasn't even got married yet."

"Well now madam, we mustn't have Matt Hancock's Granny having difficulties in my store. How would you like it if I devote some time with you to enhance your shopping experience with us?"

"That would be most helpful, but I have not told you that I am Matts Granny, have I?"

"No, I quite understand madam, now do you have a list, and I will escort you to your desired location for you to pick up the items you require."

Fawning, Millicent loved fawning, and she had no intention of correcting his assumption.

She passed the list to him and he read it quickly.

"Please, let me lead the way, and you follow me at a safe distance."

Millicent grinned and as he turned, so she followed.

They arrived at the cheese shelf, and he picked up a pack of cheddar cheese and went to put it into her basket.

"Just one moment Mr Grinton, there are three different packs here. Is that the cheapest one?"

"No madam, it isn't, but I assumed that you would be buying the best."

"Tell me Mr Grinton, does each pack proclaim to have come from Cheddar itself?"

"I have no idea madam, but I can check for you," he said as he read the outside packaging.

She watched as he picked up each brand, then said, "None of them say that it was made in Cheddar, but it must have been to have 'Cheddar' on the outside."

"So, the pack you are holding Mr Grinton is no different to the other two you are holding."

"Well technically no, but I am sure the more expensive one must be better quality. Perhaps a little more aged?"

"Ah yes, and it says this on the package outside does it?"

He looked at the packs, looking incredibly stressed. "Um, no it doesn't madam," he said, adjusting his mask.

"Then as we have established that they are all the same, I will take the lower priced item. Having moved down here recently from London, I find it tiresome to sort out all these discrepancies on pricing."

"You moved to Cheltenham from London. Well welcome to our humble store. I am sure you will find it just as helpful as the store you shopped in when you were in London."

"Mr Grinton, I never shopped in stores. I had servants to do that. This virus has put a stop on those things, and as I said to Matt as I left to come here, this non-Granny must look after herself."

"Well Madam, you are not alone, I am here to help you. Please call me Paul, and how may I address you?"

"Madam is quite sufficient Mr Grinton, we have not been formally introduced, and so we shall not break the protocols of class. You are most helpful; shall we proceed to our next port of call."

"Certainly, Madam," he said almost bowing now as he turned and walked along the aisle to the wine racks.

He stopped at the red wine and took down a bottle of Malbec.

"This is one of our very best wines, it is a little higher priced, but quality always is don't you agree."

"What is the country of origin?"

"It is Argentinian, Madam. At £12.99 a bottle it is a snip."

"And the Chilian one a little along from that one, what price is that?"

"That is priced at £5.99 Madam but will not be as good as the one I selected for you."

"Mister Grinton, was the wine in your hand pressed by the locals with their bare feet, were the grapes bigger than the ones pressed by the Chilean vintners? I think not. Place two bottles of the Chilean Malbec in my basket and then we can move on."

It was a crestfallen manager who put the selected wine back and took two of the bottles she had selected into the wheeled basket.

He adjusted himself and said, "Canned goods are this way. If you will follow me."

Millicent followed him but made a play of struggling with the trolly basket.

He soon left her behind.

He stopped at the canned goods and looked around.

Seeing Millicent coming along the aisle slowly, he rushed back to her and said, "Please Madam, let me help you with the trolly. Allow me to push it and if I go slowly, you will be able to keep up with me. I do apologise for being so thoughtless."

He took the trolly and then made his way down towards the canned goods.

Betty came up behind her and called out to her, "Millicent, where is your trolly?"

"In front of me Betty, I have the manager pushing it. He insisted he should do it."

"Oh Millicent, this is another story for you to tell us at the bridge club when we can get together. I am dying to hear all about it."

Millicent stopped at the tins on display and the manager asked Betty to please pass quickly and not to stop near this lady.

Betty pulled her mask down quickly and made a face at Millicent as she looked back, and Millicent winked back.

She was really enjoying her shopping today.

You have baked beans on your list. Any particular brand you would like Madam?

He was learning.

"I have the lowest cost you have. Your fair trade is good enough."

"I must ask Madam, could it be that we might be supplying you with something like caviar. Do you get that sent down from London?"

"I haven't had caviar since I moved down

here. The problem is of course that one is never sure of the quality."

"We do have some jars, but if you are not interested, then we can deal with the beans."

"Is it Beluga?" asked Millicent.

"No, but I am sure you will find it almost as good."

"I have paid eighty-four pounds for a small jar of Beluga, yours is at what cost?"

"£12.99, its red caviar."

"So, its Salmon eggs not the true black sturgeon eggs. I don't think so Mr Grinton. One can lower one's standard but not to those extremes."

Mr Grinton turned to the baked beans. He sighed and looked up wards. What have I done to deserve this, he thought?

"Mr Grinton, the beans," reminded Millicent as he stood holding the shelves.

He turned slowly and said, "The lowest cost baked beans, fair trade I think you said."

"Correct. They all have haricot beans inside, with tomato sauce around them. I see no point in paying high prices for similar items. Supermarkets make far too much profit from people such as I."

He looked at the list and said "Four," as he looked at her, and put them into the basket. The same with the rest of the items of tin goods was at the lowest cost.

He looked again at the list and made to move away.

"Mr Grinton, you did check each tin to see if any dents were in them, didn't you?"

"I, ah, no I didn't Madam."

"Kindly do so now then please. I want intact tins, with no dents in them."

He took each tin out, turned it checked it then put it back in the trolly basket but in a new place.

"They are all perfect Madam," he said.

"Very good. Shall we continue?"

"Eggs are this way Madam." He was beginning to sound quite weary.

They arrived at the area with eggs stacked in various bays.

"At what price level are you looking at here Madam."

"Your best price for a quantity of half a dozen."

He moved along the racks and brought back a box of six.

As he went to put them into the trolly, she said, "Are they brown or white?"

"I don't know Madam, but you only eat what is inside the shell, and an egg is an egg, is it not?"

"It is a point of view; however, I sort the eggs out and only take the brown eggs. If the hen has bothered to lay brown and white eggs, it must be that it wants us to have a choice. I prefer the brown eggs and not the white."

Paul Grinton looked at the mixed eggs in the box and returned to the rack with the egg box.

He began to look in every box to find six eggs that were all brown.

Boxes began to be stacked on the floor around the manager.

Finally, he found one, and then replaced all the boxes from the floor around him that had been rejected.

Getting up from his knee, he advanced to Millicent and with the box open, showed her the six brown eggs.

"Thank you, Mr Grinton, did you check that they were all perfect. I wouldn't like to take home a cracked egg. So unhygienic, I am sure you will agree."

"No Madam, but I will do so now."

He opened the box again, took each egg out and examined it, with over exaggeration, then replaced it in the box. Once done he placed the box into the trolly.

"For future reference Mr. Grinton, you could have swopped eggs from one box to another, to save time."

Mr Grinton looked to the ceiling, then took a deep breath. He wasn't going to say a word, no mater how much he wanted too.

They moved on around, stopping for the rest of Millicent's shopping, and at last, he said, "That is your list completed Madam."

"Well Mr Grinton, I must say, it has been a pleasure shopping here today. You have been most helpful. If you could escort me to the checkout, I will pay and be on my way."

Mr Grinton pushed the trolly to a checkout that was closed. He stacked the items onto the conveyor belt, then pushed the empty trolly basket to the till end.

He then opened the enclosure, and started the till up, putting in his own pass number.

As the shopping moved down towards the till, another person went to put her things on the conveyor, requesting a bar to separate her items from Millicent's shopping.

Mr Grinton called out to her, "I am sorry, I am just checking out this ladies items, then I will close the till again. Please try any of the other tills."

As the lady put the things back into her trolly basket she said, "Blimee, who's she then, the queen?"

Millicent smiled behind her mask and said to herself, 'That's close enough.'

Once everything was paid for and packed in Millicent's bags, Mr Grinton pushed the trolly to Betty's car, and bid Millicent goodbye.

"Please give my absolute best regards to Mr Hancock when next you speak to him. I am sure he will be pleased that we have looked after his granny."

"I will do so," said Millicent as she watched him turn and walk away, then said, "but it will have to wait until I next put my television on."

Authors note

If you enjoyed this short story of Millicent, you may like to know that next year, an adult book featuring Millicent will be published hopefully next year. This will be a full-length story and she will cause just as much chaos as in this story.

Sally's Way

Chapter one

She was a comely wench most people said.
She worked hard for her parents in the
potato fields and helped pull the hand cart to
the market each week in Winterbourne.

When her mother died, her workload
increased as she took over the job of looking
after her father.

Now they were sacking up potatoes ready for
the Winterbourne market.

Winterbourne had been granted the right to
hold a market one day per week by the king,
and two fairs in any year, to be held in June and
October.*

Her head seemed to turn for no man, other
than for Ezra Bisp.

Whenever she and her father went to the
market in the village, he was there with his
father.

He worked on the High street in the Smithy's
and on market days, people came to buy pots
or pans they had made for folk to buy.

He was a striking lad, wide of shoulder and
bulging arm muscles that echoed his strength.

He never seemed to notice her; he was far
too busy arranging the wares for best viewing.

His father would guide him, calling this way
or that, and soon the wagon was unloaded, and
they sat down on a bucket that had been made

in their forge.

Her father left her as he made his way to the George and Dragon, a wooden structure with a proud name but was at best, an ale house at the cross roads, and at worst, where women who had no other way to earn, plied their trade selling their bodies.

It was an age-old trade, and at seventeen, Sally knew of it.

Sally started to unload the cart that her father and she had pulled from their homestead. This was halfway between Yonder and Winterbourne in *Claystairs.

She heaved out the first sack of potatoes and undid the twine at the neck of the sack.

As she turned to take the next sack, a voice said, "Let me take them out of your cart, you rest now for you have had a long trek with this load from the bottom of Claystairs."

Sally looked at the man in front of her and watched as he flexed his arms and lifted the next potato bag with seemingly no effort at all.

He lowered the sack and continued to empty the cart.

Once it was unloaded, he smiled at Sally and said, "I will load into your cart any spuds you have left and will ask that your eyes will look kindly on mine."

Sally was all flustered but trying to not let this show said, "I shall welcome your hands to help me Ezra, and I will look kindly to your help. My father takes ale in the Dragon's arms and leaves me to set our pitch."

Ezra smiled and said, "I thank you Sally, and

hope that your father's cart will be less full than when you started."

He turned and walked away as other carts and drays began to arrive.

Her father returned and moved a sack of potatoes to sit on.

Sally rolled the back of her sacking skirt into a ball making sure her legs were not exposed like the working girls in the pub, and then sat on the floor waiting for a sale.

People came and went, and sacks were sold to servants who were charged to buy for the Lords and Ladies of the surrounding areas.

Local people came with baskets and bought a farthing worth of potatoes, but as her father often said, "Money, big or small, is still money."

As the market day came to an end, Sally looked at the sacks and turned to her father. "It has been a good day with our sales, father. One full sack you are sat on and short of half on the other."

"Get the cart loaded then girl, I need a small ale before I return. Here, take this farthing and see if yonder butcher has meat bones that we can put in the pot tonight."

"Will you stay to watch the cart father, for I cannot be in both places and not all are goodly folk."

"Away with you girl, get to the butcher, I will stay and watch the stall."

Picking up an open woven basket, Sally ran down the stalls clutching her coin. Meat, it had been a long time since the last time they had tasted anything as good.

She came to the butcher who was wrapping the meat into sacks to go on the horse drawn cart.

"Well young lady, what can we do to please thee?"

"Sir, my father has given me a farthing to buy some meaty bones. Please tell me that you still have such to sell."

"A treat is it that you are after? Then I shall sort a measure for you."

She watched as he lifted a barrel from the cart and lifted the wooden lid.

He dipped in his hands and said, "A farthing you say. No doubt you will be expecting a lot for such a sum."

"If it would please you Sir, then my father and I will praise your generous nature this night as we gnaw the bones."

Hand me your basket little one, for I have had a good day, and will share my bounty.

Sally passed the basket and watched as the hand came from the barrel with bones blood red and meat still showing on them.

He placed the handful of bones in her basket, and then dipped into the barrel again.

He brought out another hand full and forced them into the basket.

Blood oozed through the woven strands of the wicker basket as he handed it back to her.

She reached over with the coin, and the butcher thanked her as he took her coin.

Turning, she ran back through the bustling crowd clearing their pitches and packing their wares.

As she arrived, she saw that her father was no longer sat on the last sack of potatoes and two lads were helping themselves from the bag.

Sally arrived and swung the basket round and it hit the nearest lad on the back of his head. As he fell forward, he dropped the potatoes.

The second lad came towards her and she dropped her basket and readied herself to hit, kick and bite. No one was going to steal from her!

The lad dropped the potatoes, then with a fist raised, advanced towards her.

But she didn't do anything, for suddenly, the thief was yanked backward, and a huge hand lifted him from the ground.

Ezra holding the collar of the youths coat said, "Do I need to turn you and your senseless friend here upside down to shake the money from you, or shall we call the Sheriff's men to deal with you both for theft?"

"I'll pay, put me down."

Ezra dropped him to the floor and said to the other who was rubbing his head, "And do you want the Sheriffs men to come?"

"No, no. It was a mistake; we were just sorting out the best spuds. We were going to pay."

"Then pay the girl and pick up your spuds."

They both got to their feet and pulled out a farthing.

Each paid her the money, picked up the fallen potatoes and with a sullen glance at them both, went on their way.

"Remind me to stay on your best side Sally,

for you are mighty fearsome in a brawl."

"I thank you Ezra for your help. I must load the cart before my father returns from the ale house, for there he must be."

"Aye, and mine shall be with him no doubt."

"Then Ezra, if you would do one other small thing for me, I will be ever grateful.

"What is your wish of me, Sally?"

"Pick up the full sack of potatoes and put it into my cart, I can lift the half sack once this is done."

He picked up the sack her father had sat on and placed it into the hand cart. Sally lifted the half sack and put that in. Then she picked up her basket of bones, seeing one on the ground, she picked that up also, and put it in with the rest.

"Sally, I need to say something, for I am fair to bursting to say it."

"Then say it."

"Sally, I am getting old, and at nineteen, my time has come to find me a girl to take as a wife. Truth to tell, I have watched thee each time you come to market, and you are a girl that sets my heart afire. My father said that no man could do better than lay his heart at your feet, for you work hard, and nary a grumble comes from your lips."

Sally said nothing, but her heart was beating faster.

Ezra continued, "If thee has a mind to it, I should like to say that thee and I are betrothed, and there's an end to it."

Sally still said nothing, but stared at Ezra, who was moving from one leg to the other, looking at her, anxiously waiting for her reply.

"Ezra, I have looked at thee. Seeing you, did please my eyes."

Ezra stopped moving and gave out a great sigh.

Sally continued, "If we are to be wed, then where shall we make a home. The Sheriff must agree our union and grant us a holding if we are to farm crops."

"But Sally, I know nothing of farming. Would you not move in with my family? There is space enough to build a small adjoining home. You could work the bellows and keep the fires hot as my father and I work."

"'Tis not that I don't like thy offer Ezra, but I work the land. We shall part for now, and I will speak to my father, and you can speak to thine."

Ezra was a mixture of thoughts as he went back to his father's dray and finished loading the unsold items on it.

Sally pulled her skirt between her legs and sat on a large stone used to tether a horse, making sure her legs were covered. She didn't look at Ezra as he took hold of the horses bit and led it out onto the Bristol road.

As he turned the corner, he looked over the horse to see if Sally was watching him, but she still sat as he had left her. With a heavy heart he led the horse on the road towards the Smithy along the High street.

Sally sat for an age until her drunken father staggered up to her and said, "Girl, I knew I could count on you, so I took my leave to have a tankard of ale with my fellows."

"I know father," she said standing up, "will you be helping me pull the cart, or am I on my own with this also?"

"Now then girl, less of your lip. Here, you take one side, and I will take the other, and we will soon be in our home."

And without another word between them, they lugged the cart back along the tracks down to their holding at Claystairs.

Her father lifted the half sack of potatoes and said, "Take the sack around to the shed, I will pick a few potatoes to go into the pot, then you can collect this sack and put it with the other."

Sally lifted the full sack and dragged it to the shed. Storing it on top of logs to keep them dry, she returned to the front door, where the half sack had been placed.

She lifted this, returned to the shed and placed this on logs also. She then pulled the panel, that formed a door across the entrance and tied the strings to keep it in place.

Returning to the house, she found her father laying on his palliasse.

"I need to rest daughter; it has been a hard day's work. Wake me when the supper is cooked."

He then sat up and said, "Did you get the meaty bones I sent you to get?"

"I did father, and me and Ezra saved our potatoes from being stolen by two youths, after you left before I returned."

He sank back onto the straw mattress and closed his eyes. "He's a good lad that Ezra.

Now then, get on with cooking the feast, and put some herbs in it that you are so fond of collecting, for I do declare, thee makes a sumptuous stew, there is no doubt about it."

The fire was out but still hot, so with a small amount of kindling, she soon had it alight.

She built the fire up, then put fresh water into the mixture left from yesterday's meal. Nothing was wasted.

Sally took the small bucket out to the stream that made its way down towards the Frome river.

She filled the bucket, then returned to the house. Sitting on a small stool, she cleaned the potatoes, then cut them into small chunks.

The cauldron of vegetables from yesterday, was now swung over the fire, and she put the diced potatoes into the combination.

Next, she picked up her basket of bones and dropped them into the cauldron. It didn't make a difference about the one that had dropped on the mud, she or her father would never notice.

A rotting turnip that had been discarded, now drew her attention, and she started to cut away the rot, until she had some sound vegetable.

She washed the solid root and diced it and put it into her pot.

She pulled a small box out from the corner and took out some herbs. She chopped them up and added them to the mixture.

Now it was just a waiting game.

Her father was asleep, she listened to his snores as she sat thinking of Ezra's offer.

She was confused, she had wanted him to

catch her eye, but when he had spoken to her of a union, she had almost said no to him, if her farming days were to be over. What to do?

Sally mulled over the problem until after one or two tastes, she declared it was ready. She had spooned a bone to the top and pulled a strip of meat from it. It was delicious.

Pulling the two wooden bowls from a shelf, she called to her father that supper was ready.

He woke and looked at her, struggling to sort out where he was.

"Ah, daughter, have you created your magic once again?"

"Tis cooked well enough father, and if you sit to the table, I will bring some to you."

She scooped out the vegetables and a large bone and handed it to her father.

"One bone to gnaw on, nay girl, give me three. It has been a hard day's work today. A man must eat heartily after such a day's work."

Sally said nothing but got up and took another wooden bowl and fished out two more bones. She placed them by her father's plate and sat to eat her own meal.

Once the meal was over, and the bowls had been licked clean, she took them and the bones out of the house and swilled them in the stream.

Next, she put the bones into a box in the shed, they would be broken up tomorrow and any marrow would end up in the pot for tomorrow.

She returned to the house, wiping the bowls on her apron, then put them onto the shelf.

Her father returned to his bed and lay once

again on it.

Sally wanted to talk to him about Ezra, but it wouldn't be tonight.

"Don't waste a candle, get yourself into thy bed. You have worked well this day daughter, and now you must rest. We have work to do tomorrow."

She pulled the cauldron away from the fire and put a grid around it to stop any half-burnt logs falling out.

Sally went out of the house, walked a short way away from it. She looked around and seeing no one, squatted down and eased her bladder.

Returning to the dwelling, she pulled the door shut, then put the wooden bar across to lock it in place.

Her father was asleep, and she went to her straw mattress and sank down on it.

The dwelling had no rooms, everything was in the one room.

She had no shoes on her feet, and there being no point in changing her clothes as the gentry did, she was told. She pulled the coarse blanket over her, and soon joined her father in sleep.

Chapter Two

Sally woke before her father and throwing off the blanket, got up from her bedding and then rolled it up. She tied string to it, then lifted it onto the storage shelf ready for this evening.

She took the slats out, then lifted the frame

up against the wall.

Stoking the fire, she found it still had heat, so she put kindling on and soon had a fire going again.

Struggling with the weight, she lifted the cauldron from the hook, and put on a smaller version of it.

It now waited for the breakfast to be put into it.

Having removed the bar to the door, she went outside and went to the shed.

She took the wooden ladle down from the side of the frame and opened a sack of ground wheat. She took a scoop and put it in the small wooden bowl that was also handy for this purpose.

Returning to the house, she set the bowl down. She picked up an earthenware jug and left the house to walk up to Yonder, the hamlet bordering their home.

Here she purchased an egg and a jug of milk for her farthing.

Returning to her home, she mixed the ground wheat with the egg, added some milk. She took two cooked potatoes from the stew and crushed these into the mixture.

She stirred this, then scraped it into the smaller cauldron, then pushed it over the fire.

Her father began to stir as the breakfast contents began to bubble.

Unwrapping a damp cloth, she took a part used loaf of bread, and cut large chunks from it.

Her father sat up, itched his vast stomach, then swung his legs out onto the mud floor.

He pushed his feet into the old leather sandals, looking almost as black as his feet.

Her mother had found them discarded and the strap broken, but she had resewn them and whilst not perfect, made her father look a little more presentable.

She drew the small cauldron from the fire and taking two wooden bowls, pulled the thick stodgy food from the cauldron.

Sally passed her father his and a chunk of bread.

She placed hers on the table and then sat with her father who was already devouring his meal.

Sally ate hers slowly, thinking how she should tell her father about the offer of wedlock from Ezra.

"Eat up girl, we have work to do this day, and you will need your belly full."

"I need to tell thee something of importance father, and I would beg thee to hear my say."

"Say it then daughter, for times wasting."

"Ezra has asked me to become his wife."

"Good, I hope you said yes, this place could do with a strong hand come digging time."

"He wants me to live with him at the forge, to give up farming."

"What's to become of me if this were to happen. I need you to be with me since your mother did die."

"He won't give up his smithy job father."

"Then that's an end to it. He stays at the forge, and you stay here. I will hear no more about it. Now finish the breakfast and get to work.

She ate her meal, then tidied up the bowls and went out to join her father.

A tree that had been partly cut down for firewood, still had the roots and some left over higher branches to be cut. They needed to cut down the remaining branches and then dig the tree roots out.

A ladder was propped against the tree, and the bow saw was waiting to be hauled up to the branches to be cut.

"Up you go girl. I will steady the ladder for you, then once you are ready, get sawing that big branch up there," he said pointing.

Sally climbed the ladder and onto the tree branch.

She pulled up the bow saw, then standing as best she could, started to cut through the branch.

After many stops to rest and drink some water, also to come down to relieve her bladder, the branch was showing signs of dropping as each cut was made.

A rope was thrown up to Sally and she tied it to the branch so that her father could guide its fall.

Sally restarted sawing when she heard someone calling.

As the branch started to sag, and the cut opened even more, it became easier.

With a will, Sally increased her strokes and again the branch sagged.

"Almost done now father she shouted," as she positioned herself to make the last few cuts.

Then she looked down and saw her father

below her and he was laughing at Ezra.

Ezra was angry, she could see that, and he stepped closer to her father.

Sally moved her weight and as it pressed onto the sawn branch, so it gave.

The branch went crashing down and hit her father as he looked up.

Ezra moved back just in time to avoid it.

Sally came down from the tree, and once on the ground, looked at her prone father.

The branch had hit his head and he was beneath the branch. His eyes stared up at her, as she sank to the ground.

She knew he was dead; no one could live with one side of his head crushed in.

Tears rolled down her eyes as she looked at him, afraid to touch him, not knowing what to do.

Ezra sank down beside her. He rested an arm on her back. As she cried over her father, she was not even aware of his touch.

They stayed like this for a while, and as people passed and saw something was amiss, they came to see what help they could offer.

When the Sheriff came, everyone moved for him to see.

"Well now, an accident I am told." He looked up at the tree, then down to the branch and the rope.

"Did any other see this happen?"

Ezra stood and said, "I did Sheriff. I was talking to her father when the branch gave way. I jumped away, but he took the full force of it. I have but a few cuts and grazes."

"Then, I shall record it in my book that it was death by an accident, and you had best get some strong lads to cut the branch up to get the body out," he said to Ezra. "Before you go, and for my records, it must be said in public, Ezra Bisp are you a witness to this accident?"

"Yes Sheriff, I am."

"And you Sally Ricks, are you a witness to this accident?"

"Yes," said Sally, as she wiped her nose on her sleeve.

"And this is your father, Edgar Ricks, lying dead before me?"

"He is," said Sally.

"Then I am done here. The church won't grant you a burial in the holy grounds, best you find a place to bury him, he's likely to start smelling soon if you wait. You will need to come to my house to formally ask if you can stay in the homestead, and to continue your farming. This must be done in ten days, or you will be evicted."

The Sheriff mounted his horse and rode away.

Over the next few hours, the big branch was cut up and her father picked up and laid on the ladder.

He was taken to their home and placed on the floor.

Sally took the blanket down and rolled him into it, then tied it around him.

"Do you have money for the priest to say some words?" asked Ezra.

"No, we laid my mother in a grave we made down by the river."

"Then we can put your father by her side."

"That would be good."

She turned to the other young man who had helped bring him into their home and said, "I think Ezra and I had better see father on his way. You know what the Sheriff is like. He won't be best pleased to know my parents rest on the edge of the Barons land."

The young man nodded and wished them well as he left.

Ezra lifted her father up and Sally pushed the ladder under him. They adjusted his feet to balance him, and then tied a rope around the ladder and the body.

Sally went to the shed, took out two spades, and lay them on top of her father's body.

Ezra went to the front, bent down, and took hold of the short ladder. Sally did the same with the other end.

They came out of the house and walked down towards the river.

Reaching the riverbank, they walked along the edge towards the bridge known as Damson bridge.

The foliage covered land sloped steeply towards the river.

They struggled along and at last came to a slightly open area, and Sally said, "This is it."

They lowered the ladder, and then Sally marked the area to dig.

"I will stand this side and did. Mother is underneath me, but she won't mind me standing on her."

She started to dig, and Ezra joined her from

the other side.

It wasn't a very deep hole, but it didn't need to be.

They untied her father, and laid him down into the ground, still wrapped in the blanket.

Sally slipped the sandals from his feet and set them aside.

She then stood looking at her father.

"Well father, you are with mother now, I must make my own way in this world now, rest well."

She shovelled the first pile of earth onto the body and as she did the second lot, Ezra shovelled earth from his side. Soon the mound was banked up and she picked up two sticks and laid them on the mound in a shape of a cross.

Ezra came and stood by her as she stood at the foot of the grave.

She turned to Ezra and said, "Come on Ezra, give me a hand with the ladder, I need to get back to the homestead."

She picked up the sandals and lifted up the front part of the ladder. It was easier to manoeuvre it through all the brush carrying between them, rather than Ezra try on his own.

As they walked back, Sally thought about her father and Ezra below her talking and looking angry.

Ezra put the ladder against the shed and said, "Twernt my fault he died Sally. I was asking him about me and you. He got angry about it, and said you had to look after him. The branch just fell on us. Nought I could do to save him."

"I know Ezra, it's a bad time though. I have

seven more rows of spuds to lift, and I need to see the Sheriff to see if he's going to evict me."

"Would you like me to come with you? I will if you wish."

"My thanks Ezra, but I must do this alone if I am to continue farming. Unless you called to say you want to join me."

"No, Sally. Much as I would like to, I can't."

"Then I must thank thee for all you have done, and I will see thee on the next market day, and that's an end to it."

"So be it, Sally. Know this, I will always watch out for you, no matter what you say."

He turned and walked up the pathway and soon was lost from her sight.

She slept fitfully that night but woke determined to start on what would be her own plot of land to farm.

Sally got some water and washed her face and hands. Lifting her apron, she dried her self.

Next, she lifted the stone at the side of the shed and picked up her father's coin bag. She slipped it into her apron pocket.

She set off up the walkway towards the main roadway, then turned and took the path across the common towards the Mount.

Once she came to Flaxpits lane, she crossed over and made her way towards the High street. As she reached this, in front of her was the Sheriffs house.

She crossed the two-track roadway and walked to the gateway.

A soldier was standing by the entrance and asked her what her business was.

"I have come to see the Sheriff as he requested me to do so."

"Name?"

Sally gave him her name.

"Wait here, I will see if he has time for the likes of you."

He shut the gate and went to the door. After knocking it, another soldier came out and they spoke quietly to each other.

The soldier returned and said, "Wait here, the sheriff is a busy man, and may not see you today."

She stood away from the gate and waited.

It seemed a long time before the second soldier came to the gate.

"The Sheriff will see you now. Follow me."

She went through the gate and then through the front door, following the soldier.

Finally, he stopped and knocked the door.

"Come," was the reply.

The soldier opened the door and waved her in. Once she had moved away from the door, he shut it and she was stood watching the Sheriff reading some papers. They looked old and were brown and crackled as he moved them.

"You have come to ask about your fathers holding at the bottom of Claystairs."

"Yes Sir, as you instructed me to do this, so I am here."

"As I see. Well Sally Ricks. The lease is in the name of Edgar Ricks, not yours. I am afraid I must evict you."

"Oh no. Please Sir, let me stay, I can work the

land as well as my father did, and pay the levy on time as he did."

"Do you live with a man?"

"No Sir, no man has claimed my body for a marriage."

"You know the rules Sally Ricks. No woman can claim a homestead without a man giving his mark of agreement."

"But there must be some way you can help me."

"Well." He paused watching her take a deep breath in the hope of an idea to help.

"Please Sir, anything."

"You said anything. Well Sally Ricks, lay with me and give me pleasure with all your young body can give, and I, in return will give you papers to find a man within one year and one day. If you fail to find him. Then you must leave. Refuse my offer, and you have five days to pack up and leave."

"And if I do this thing, you will give me the paper with the grant of one year?"

"Yes."

Sally thought about it for quite a while. She looked at the Sheriff, a man of much older age than she. He was rotund, with fleshy jowls, not the man she would wish for to be her first.

She then thought of the girls who did this thing for pence in the pub.

"When would you want this to be done?"

"Now," he said pointing to the corner of the room to a cot. "My bed is over there."

"And when this act is done, will you give me the paper to say I have one year and one day to homestead my farm area."

"After you have gone, I will draw up the paperwork and sign it. One of my men will come to your homestead and announce that you have the year to remain in the homestead, but only that. Then he will nail it to your door."

"Why not give me the paper after you..." She didn't like to say what was going to happen.

"It has got to be a public announcement. That makes your stay legal."

She stood there quietly thinking, then making up her mind, walked over to the makeshift bed.

Behind her back, the Sheriff grinned.

He followed her to the bed and said, "Are we in agreement then."

Sally looked at the floor. "Yes."

"Then take off your clothes, I want to look at you."

Sally turned her back to him and untied the cords to her neckline on her sacking dress. She untied the apron and pulled it over her head. Then she paused.

Behind her, the Sheriff held his breath.

Sally then bent down, took the bottom of her dress, and pulled it up over her head.

The Sheriff behind her gasped as her bottom came into view.

She gathered the rest of the dress and removed it totally. She was now naked.

She stayed with her back to him.

"Turn around, slowly."

She didn't do this at once, but then she started to turn. Once she was facing him, she stopped and stood before him.

"Lovely. I knew you had a wonderful body under your rags. Now, lay on the bed, and I will disrobe, then we can seal our bargain."

She did as he bid, not saying a word.

Soon he was naked and knelt on the foot of the bed, pushing his knee between her legs.

He looked up her body, watching her breasts rise and fall. She had gripped each side of the mattress and her head was turned to the side looking across the room.

"Come now girl, you have seen your mother and father couple. You know what is required of you."

Still she did not look at him, but she opened her legs and felt him move up between them.

He lay on her and she could feel his manhood pressing on her inner most part.

She clenched her teeth as he mauled her breasts saying, "I knew you had a goodly pair on you."

Then she felt him pushing his hand between her legs and he moved his position before he pushed himself sharply into her.

She shouted as he drove into her, then worked his body back and forward whilst the pain of the intrusion, rose and fell. She felt as if she was being torn apart.

And finally, he gasped, his fowl breath going straight into her face, as he discharged his seed into her.

Still she stared at the wall across the room.

She felt him move from her, and he climbed from the bed leaving her laying there.

"Right Sally Ricks, you can dress again now.

You have given yourself to me, and you will
get your just rewards. My man will call on you
in the morning and deliver the paperwork to
you."

Sally closed her legs and swung around on
the bed placing her feet on the ground as she sat
up.

She stood up, turned her back on the
Sheriff and bent to pick up her clothes she had
dropped on the floor.

She sorted her dress out, lifted it above her
head and let it drop down over her nakedness.
She slipped the apron over her head and tied it
behind her.

Then she turned to see the Sheriff sat once
again at his desk.

He looked up at her as she stood there.

"You can go now Sally Ricks. Our business is
done. My man will call tomorrow as agreed.
Good day to you."

She turned and walked to the door, then
opened it and went out.

The soldier was sitting outside, and he looked
at her and gave a grin.

"Follow me," he said.

He led her out and then she was soon passing
through the gateway and out onto the roadway.

Wagons were passing as she watched and
once a gap came, she crossed the rutted
roadway.

She made her way back to the homestead
and fetched a small bucket from inside.

She then went to the small stream and filled it
with water.

Sally returned to her home and shut the door.

A small amount of light filtered in as she took her clothes off and taking a coarse cloth, washed her body parts that had been invaded with vigour. She felt sick.

She washed every part of her body, clearing the months of ingrained dirt and the touch of the odious Sheriff.

Once she was satisfied, she opened the door and threw the soiled water out.

She pulled out a 'go to church' dress and pulled this on, then took the bucket and got more water.

Back at her home, she put the dress into the small, now clean cauldron, and poured water over it.

Then she pushed it over the fire still warm from the morning and stoked it up with new logs.

Soon it was boiling, and she swung it away from the fire and stirred it around watching the dirt come out from it.

Once she was happy with it, she left it to soak, and climbed onto her bed.

She cried herself into a fitful sleep.

Chapter Three

Sally woke early and sorted out the dress she had cleaned.

She pushed her rumpled dress down and went out to put her work dress on a bush to dry.

She sat at the door of her homestead and

waited for the Sheriff's man to come and read the proclamation that she could stay for another year.

She heard the sound of hoofs before she saw the soldier arrive. She stood and watched him dismount and take a rolled piece of paper out of his tunic.

"Hear yeah one and all. The Sheriff has this day signed and given notice that this homestead held in the name of the dead keeper, Edgar Ricks, shall after five days be declared vacant and a notice of eviction to one Sally Ricks, female living here is now served. All those who wish to take up this homestead should make his name known to the Sheriff."

He then turned to Sally and said, "Five days, then we will arrest you if you are not gone. Take all that is yours, but do not damage the Lords property."

"But the Sheriff said that he would give me a year to find a husband. This cannot be right."

"You know the law girl. No female can hold any rights to property other than through her husband or any other who lives with her and she obeys. As I look at thee, I can see you are a female. You have been served the notice, be as quick as you can girl."

Tears ran down her eyes as the soldier nailed the paper to her front door.

People who had listened, drifted away, they hated to see this, but could do little to help her.

Sally sat on a chair by the door and let her tears fall on her 'going to church dress.'

Her thoughts started to focus on the one

thing. She had been cheated by the Sheriff and had lost two things she had treasured the most. Now she was no better than the inn girls, and without a means to live, this seemed to be her only way to earn money.

As she thought about it, so she was sick, vomiting between her legs in front of the door.

This seemed to make her decide on what to do next.

She got water and flushed the bile away, then shut her door and marched up the walkway on the common. She cut across the common and came to the High street. Turning left, she made her way to the smithy.

On arrival, she called out to Ezra and asked if he could spare a moment.

His father nodded to him and Ezra came from the smithy, hot, sweaty, and stripped to the waist.

"What is it Sally? Only we be fearsome busy with a special order for the Lord of the Mount."

"I have been given notice to leave the homestead Ezra, and I shall need your help. That is if you be willing to help me."

"Aye Sally, I told thee you could count on me and so you shall. I will call down to your home and we shall talk then."

"I have five days Ezra, and today is one of them."

"I shall come Sally, never fear."

He turned and went back to his work, and Sally started her walk back to the homestead.

Once there, she gathered the empty sacks up, and then went inside the house, changed back into her working dress, tied the apron on and went to the first row of potatoes that needed lifting.

She toiled through the day, stopping only to get a chunk of bread and some water from the brook.

By the end of the day, she had all the potatoes in the sacks, and she shuffled her way to her home, and sat with the door open waiting.

Ezra came as he promised, and he pulled out a chair and sat beside her.

"What a mess Sally. Now what's to do?"

"Ezra, I think before anything else be said between thee and I, you should be told of something that may make your eyes stop looking at me as they do."

"Pray tell me Sally, for nothing can be so bad that cannot be sorted out."

And so, she told him the whole sequence of events. As she told him about the invasion of her body, she watched as the muscle on his cheek flexed as he gritted his teeth. His hands were clenched, and he was clearly angry.

Finally, she came to the deceitfulness of the Sheriff.

She turned and looked at him.

He was shaking his head and said nothing to her as she stood and went into her home.

Sally pulled out a box and opened it.

She picked up her father's sandals and put them into the box. Next, she pulled down her father bedding and rolled that into a small enough shape that it could go into the box.

Sally continued with her packing, leaving her own bed ready to sleep in.

She put small pots into bigger ones and soon had two piles. Not noticeably big, but easy to manage.

Ezra stood and turned to her.

She stopped her work and looked at him.

"Tis a stupid thing that thee has done, but I cannot see my way without you."

She started to move toward him, and he lifted his hand palm towards her to stop her.

"Hear me first Sally, then we shall see. Twill be hard for me to look at you and think of him with thee, but me hopes that you will put this thought out of my mind with thy love for me. If you be still agreeable, then we are still betrothed, and I shall this day tell my father and mother of the good news that you will live with me."

Sally ran to him and they kissed for the first time.

He helped bring all the sacks of potatoes into the shed and lock it up. Then he said, "I must be on my way, for I wish to speak to my father and mother."

She watched him walk away and went back into her home.

Sally lay on her bed and thought about all that had happened.

Sleep came as she lay there, and morning seemed but a moment after she had slept.

Somehow, she felt better about herself.

She made a breakfast, tidied up, and then started to pack other odd bits.

She was in her house when she heard a horse outside, and fearing it was the Sheriff, hid behind the door, looking through a gap.

It was Ezra's father.

He got down from the cart and as she emerged from the dwelling, he said, "I have come to help you move. You have made my wife and I very happy, and now we have a smiling son. Come, Sally, let's pack your things onto the cart and you can turn your back on all of this."

She smiled at him, and then said, "I have most of my things packed. We did not own much, but what we have was bought honestly."

They loaded the pots, the box with her and her mother's clothes in it. She had rolled up her father's better clothes, his works clothes he was still wearing.

They then loaded the potatoes and all the other oddments. Lastly, she put her tools on the back that they used for digging and planting.

She looked around, saw nothing that she wanted so climbed on to the cart and sat beside Mr Bisp.

He clucked and shook the reigns and the horse leaned in and the cart started to move.

It was hard work for the horse to turn it around but once they were back in the ruts formed by other carts, the going got easier.

They came to the High street and soon Mr Bisp pulled up the horse and then helped her down.

They got married quite quickly and with local helpers, a new stone-built home was built adjoining the smithy.

Sally worked in the smithy, pushing the bellows as her husband worked at the forge.

Now and then, she walked down to the old homestead to take a look at the way it was being worked.

Then she would turn her back on it and walked back to her home through a narrow lane that some now call Sally's way.

Notes

*Winterbourne had been granted the right to hold a market one day per week by the king, and two fairs in a year, to be held in June and October.

In 1393 the King granted to the Lady of the manor of Winterbourne the right to hold a market day once a week and two fairs. The market was held around the crossroads of Winterbourne village.

The George and Dragon established in 1786 was the ale house that replaced the wooden structure that was the ale house Sally's father drank from in our story, set about 1742.

The fairs were held adjacent to Winterbourne Church and near manor court.

(A history of Winterbourne. H W N Ludwell)

*Claystairs

Claystairs was called this because the ground tended to have a high predominance of clay and held water. Farmers would farm crops in stairs or steps, this allowed drainage and the growing of crops that might rot in soggy soil. Claystairs is now known as Cloisters.

(A history of Winterbourne. H W N Ludwell)

The Good Samaritan

Clive Snedan sat back in his chair and studied his signature on the card he had just signed.

No doubt about it he thought, no one could copy this signature, and they couldn't even read it!

He had been prompted to sign the donor card after a programme on TV that he had watched. They needed organs, and he had been so moved by people dying because no organ was available, he was determined that he would do something about it.

He had ticked to donate everything.

He took the card and with a smile pushed it into his new wallet he had purchased a day or so ago. He glanced at the clock and pulled his coat on and with a last glance around the house, let himself out and went on his way to work. Fortunately, he was not required to be early this morning, the audit he was doing was almost finished.

At the same time, Cyril Lovely eased his feet out of bed and scratched his chest as he yawned his way into a new day.

Lovely may be his name but not his nature.

He was a tall well-built man; good looking some would say in a rugged sort of way.

There the lovely part ended, for truth to tell, Lovely was the epitome of evil. He saw no good in anything or anyone.

He had grown up as a bully spending most of his time beating fellow students for their money.

He had been excluded from school on two occasions and had even been the cause of a nervous breakdown to one of his teachers, much to his delight.

His later years had been spent in and out of prison on various charges. Theft, GBH, extortion and pimping, nothing was excluded from his repertoire.

As he pulled on his trousers he reflected on the night before.

He had taken a guy for just over £100.00 pounds. He had seen him take some money from the hole in the wall and followed him.

Once he had him near a narrow side road, he had closed up on the unfortunate man, stuck a knife into his ribs so that he could feel it and taking him by his left arm had asked him if he would like to feel the knife go right home. The man had felt the knife point and the hard grip the huge meaty hand had on his left arm.

The target had looked up at the hard-cruel face of Cyril Lovely who had with very little resistance, guided him into the narrow lane between the shops.

Lovely had cautioned him to make no sound and had guided him with the occasional prod with the knife ever deeper into the narrow and now dark lane.

Finally, he had pushed the man against the wall, his meaty hand now lying flat against the man's chest and the knife thrust under his chin. Just to remind him he had pushed up with the knife and a trickle of blood had started to run down the neck of the terrified man.

"Now then" he had said "we can do this nice and easy or I can do you in and help myself to what I want. What's it to be?"

The poor man had been unable to move as the hand at his chest had relaxed and moved into his inside coat pocket to remove the wallet, he had filled just a short time ago.

Lovely had flicked it open glanced at the bundle of notes just showing above the lip of the wallet before it was pushed into his pocket.

"Now then, so as there is no fuss as I leave you". So, saying Lovely had stepped back slightly, and slammed his huge, balled fist straight across the chin of the unfortunate man.

It had been as easy as that, he had left the man in the lane unconscious and light of pocket.

Having lost all of the money in a card game and drinks last night, he now needed a new source of finance. It worked before so why not again.

With a final scratch at his chest, he lumbered out of the flat and onto the stairs. The landlady was waiting at the foot of the stairs and demanded the back rent as he pushed passed her.

"Later" was his gruff reply as he moved out and down the steps to the pathway.

He made his way up the High street to the same hole in the wall and finding a good spot that was not too close but gave a view of the transactions done, he waited for the right sized target to come along.

It was important that his size should have some effect on the selected person, the initial fear was a big help, and by the time the shock had worn off, it was always too late.

He leaned against the wall and waited. Time passed and then he spotted his new victim.

A little runt of a man had just come up to the hole in the wall.

He could see he had drawn a good amount of cash, for the mug openly stuffed it into his wallet before turning and walking back up the High street.

Lovely pushed away from the wall and set off after his latest cash source.

Knowing he was coming up to the lane he used before, he closed on his target and eased his knife out into his hand.

Keeping it close to his side he came up to his victim, and with a strike like a cobra, pressed the knife through the man's clothes until he felt resistance.

Taking the man's arm, he gave an extra prod to reinforce the message to do as he said.

Clive Snedan was guided down the narrow lane between the shops totally unable to do anything as the monster of a man uttered "Don't do anything foolish now and you just might get to live."

A huge hand pushed him against a wall and the knife was thrust under his chin.

Clive Snedan's bladder let him down as he looked up at the brute towering above him.

The brute then said, "Just you ease out that nice fat wallet I saw you fill for me and I can be on my way."

Snedan opened his coat pocket with indecent haste and held out the wallet.

The brute took the wallet. He remembered very little from then on as a huge fist hit him on his jaw and he bounced against the wall and slowly sank to the floor.

Lovely opened the wallet flicked through the cash.

Nothing very much extra in this one, just a few stubs, the bank cash card which he dropped on the man lying on the floor, There was also a return bus ticket and a donor card, and he left that in the wallet.

It was a nice new wallet, so with nothing incriminating in it, it now his property.

With a good days work done, he retraced his steps and came out onto the High street only to bump into yesterday's victim.

He recognised Lovely as quickly as Lovely had he.

The man started to shout to everyone that he was a thief who had attacked him yesterday.

Lovely turned and ran as fast as he could barging his way through the crowds in his panic to be rid of the shouts behind him.

He turned this way and that and at last could hear no more sounds.

Looking behind him to check he was not being followed he stepped out into the road into the path of a bus.

The bus driver tried to stop, but he hit Lovely full on and lifted him into the air.

Clive Snedan opened his eyes and looked

around him. "Hello old chap, how do you feel now" a doctor asked,

"You had a nasty bang on the head, and you were concussed for a time, but I think you are now on the mend."

"How long have I been here" asked Clive.

"This is your third day. It's been a bit hectic here, but we have had our eye on you while you have been unconscious."

He went on, "We had a big rush on to contact people waiting for transplants, as a big guy who was knocked down by a bus was brought in two days ago at the same time as you, and he had signed a donor card for all organs to be used."

Clive frowned as he listened.

"We only know his name; the police have informed us he was an unbelievably bad person. But he had a donor card with him so in our books he was obviously a good Samaritan."

Clive Snedan said nothing but smiled to himself.

He remembered his thoughts a few days ago. 'No one could copy this signature, and they couldn't even read it'.

A good Samaritan indeed.

Authors note

I wrote this short story a long time ago. It is modern day but could be anywhere.

The Thief

He had been outside the big house before, looking for scraps of food to feed his family.

Others had also called as the Baron entered his home, but if he saw them, but he took no notice.

But then, one had dared to climb up into the big house and had got inside through a window.

A few hours later, his lifeless body had been thrown out through the kitchen window to land with a thud at the feet of those still searching for food scraps.

One father, desperate to gain any scrap of food, had gone into the food waste bin, and was caught picking up some rotting cheese.

They had beat him, and then chopped him in half. His dead body was then thrown into the bin to join the very food he had been trying to get.

Yes, it was a hard life to be a poor forager in this world.

But tonight, he was going to try to become a thief.

He knew that since the last attempt, by one brave sole had occurred, the Baron had got a guard to watch over the dining area, the kitchen, and the larder.

But his starving children needed food.

Our potential thief saw the lights come from the window that he knew could give him access to the areas where the food could be found.

He had to be patient.

His stomach rumbled as wonderful smells came to him from the window.

Our thief needed to see.

Deciding that just one look wouldn't be noticed, he reached up to a protruding stone and hauled himself up a small way.

Choosing the right route where the stones that would offer purchase could help him gain the sight he needed, he climbed up the wall and made it to the window ledge.

He peered over.

No one saw him.

He scrambled slightly higher and could now see inside the room.

The Baron was a filthy eater, and often seemed to speak with his mouth full.

As he watched, the Baron stuffed copious amounts of meat into his mouth with his hands, then shouted at a servant to bring more ale.

The poor man was sprayed by bits of meat flying from the Baron's mouth.

The shouting disturbed the guard who was moving towards the corner of the room. He was away from the Baron and was aware of his masters filthy habit of spraying and talking as he devoured the contents of his meal.

He had a job to do and must show willing.

The guard stopped, stretched and then, walked around the room, looking for any tale-tale signs of those who might break in and hide.

He looked behind the tall heavy drapes hanging from the window high up and down to the floor. Nothing behind the curtain.

Next, he walked behind chairs, again no sign of anything untoward.

He passed the fireplace, still burning and returned to his seat.

As the Baron gave a big belch, the guard looked at his master, seemingly in disgust, but it wouldn't do for him to see this.

With a last look around, the guard made his way back to the corner and waited patiently, but ever alert.

His master soon finished all that he could eat and bellowed for more ale.

A servant came in with a jug and poured ale into the tankard offered.

Once filled to the top, the servant retreated back to where he came from.

The thief watched all this from the window ledge, wondering if he should chance it, or return empty handed.

As he watched, the Baron heaved himself up from the chair and shakily made his way to the big armchair nearer the fire.

He placed his tankard on a small table to the side.

Taking the arms of the chair, he lowered his considerable girth into the chair, giving a tremendous fart as he did so, and before his bottom rested on the cushion.

The guard again looked at his master as the noise echoed around the room.

The Baron called out loudly again for someone to come to him, and a man new to the thief, entered the room.

"My boots, remove my books, I need to rest."

The man lifted the Barons right leg, stepped over it with his back to the Baron.

He took hold of the boot at the heel and as he pulled, the Baron put his other filthy boot onto the servants bottom and pushed.

The boot came from the foot of his master with a sucking sound.

Turning, the servant placed the removed boot by the chair, then turned, lifted the other boot stepped across the Barons leg and again presented his bottom for his master to push on.

Again, with a sucking noise, the other boot was removed and placed by the other.

No words had been spoken by the servant, and he stood facing his superior waiting for any other commands.

The Baron waved him away and snuggled down against the cushions in the chair.

Still the thief waited and watched.

Aromas of food still untouched drifted up to the window, and his stomach rumbled again.

The guard moved, had he heard the noise?

No. The thief continued to watch carefully.

The guard decided to get comfortable himself and sat on a cushion taking advantage of a rest while the Baron relaxed.

As he watched, the thief listened to the deep breathing of the Baron and this told him that he was asleep. Next his attention was drawn to the guard.

He watched as the eyes of the sentry slowly started to drift closed and as the Baron started to snore, the guards eyes finally closed.

Our thief decided to make the attempt.

Climbing through the open window, he again checked the two people who could do the most harm to him.

Both were asleep.

Catching hold of the long drape he lowered himself slowly down, and quietly inch by inch, he reached the floor.

Looking around, he checked that it was still safe.

Making his mind up that it was now or never, he quietly made his way to the abandoned table with all the food on it and using the chair that the Baron had sat on, reached the table, his target.

Great chunks of food were spread on the table, there was almost the same amount on the table as was on the platters.

He picked out juicy morsels and began stuffing his pouch with as much as he could carry.

When he was satisfied that he could put no more into the pouch, he started to make his way back.

He started his climb up the drapes. But now he was heavier and the rings holding the drapes at the top started to knock together as he made his way up to the window.

The guard opened his eyes, looked around and then jumped up and ran to the drapes.

He was making a lot of noise as he reached up to catch the thief, but he couldn't quite make it.

The thief, got to the window, squeezed through, almost bursting his pouch as he did so, and turned.

Reversing down the wall, using the uneven stones as he did before, he made it to the ground.

Looking around, making sure no horse and cart was coming, he crossed the road, ran through the hedge, and to his home.

Everyone was pleased to see the brave father mouse who had stolen cheese from the Baron and got past his guard the cat.

As he took the cheese from the pouch in his mouth and laid it in front of the family. he knew, they would all feast well this evening.

The Three Monks

The three men came into the open area, looked around and then took the loads they were carrying from their shoulders and placed them on the ground.

"I think we may have found just what we have been looking for," said one.

Another still looking around called out, "Not only a pond, but a river running close by."

The more they looked around the more they liked what they saw.

Deciding to stay, they set about finding a suitable place to build a dwelling.

There was plenty of thin saplings and sturdy Oak, Ash and Elm trees.

The men opened their bags and pulled out hand tools, saws, and a wooden mallet. One withdrew an awl for cutting holes into wood.

They found a slightly raised area between two mighty oaks and then started to cut some young sapling down.

As one brought the saplings to the area, another trimmed the small branches from the stalk and then threw it onto a growing pile.

When one of them called the others to him.

He laid a long piece of twine on the ground then did the same with a large gap between it. They arranged the sapling poles in a row along the twine then lay the trimmed poles out on the floor.

They made sure that the two outer ones were

bigger and longer than the rest, and that two were spaced in the line of poles on the floor.

Again, more twine was pulled from the bag. One tied the twine to the first pole in line with the twine under the laid-out saplings.

This was repeated with another length of twine, again in line with the second run of twine on the ground.

One of the men, took hold of the twine beneath the poles, and pulled it up into a loop.

The twine tied to the first pole was now threaded through the loop, and a loop was made on the other side and again, the top twine was passed through that. The top loose twine was now pulled back and a knot secured the two poles.

By repeating this on all the poles, they soon had a flexible wall that could bend to any shape.

They stood it up, checked it for rigidness and then started on another.

By the time the sun went down, they had four sets of the flexible wall with slight gaps in it, and a six-pole structure that was rigid as cross poles had been added.

The longer poles in the frame now had a point cut on the longer ends, giving four sharp poles to each set.

They positioned the first set beneath the boughs of the Oak trees, by bending the sets into a quadrant.

One man hammered the outside pole into the ground with his wooden mallet, then as the other two men held the frame in position, he hammered the second, third and fourth long poles into the ground.

They continued like this until the circle was complete, and the last frame overlapped slightly wider, giving a narrow gap for anyone to walk in. They brought their bags inside the dwelling and then pulled the small six pole structure into the gap, closing them inside.

A roof this evening would be the trees and the leaves.

They unpacked the bags, pulling out dried meat and stale bread, this would be their meagre meal.

A waterskin had been filled and they each drank from this.

Once they had finished, they pulled their bag to a place in the sanctuary and then lay on the ground.

Soon they were in an exhausted sleep.

The following morning, they went down to the river and bathed themselves. They then set about working again on the dwelling and found two sturdy young trees that had a single fork high up.

They felled both, the trimmed and odd branches and took both to the centre of the dwelling. They dug out a hole and pushed both trees now cut with a Y formation at the top, into the hole. They lashed both together and then replaced the soil, stamping it down firmly.

Cutting more saplings, they cleaned them up and once a pile had been formed, one man climbed up the Y fork and as a pole was passed up, he lay it in the fork and then rested the other end on the wall in the gaps.

By working around in a circle, the roof soon appeared spanning out from the centre and slightly widening on the outside edge.

Now the men picked the thinning's to weave in and out along the outer part of the roof, filling in a lot of the gaps.

It wasn't going to keep the rain out, but the men had not finished yet.

Cutting two more strong saplings. They notched the two evenly then tied short pieces going across the two taller saplings and made a ladder.

One climbed the ladder and the other two went and pulled up clods of grass from around the pond and river.

They threw this up onto the spars that made the roof, and the man on the ladder laid them on the poles radiating out. Soon the roof was covered with grass clods and mud.

They stood back and admired their work. It had been a hard toil but now they had a more permanent dwelling.

The men now talked of food, and it was decided that they should walk up the hill to the village they had seen. Maybe they could earn a bite to eat by offering their labour.

They pulled on their coarse brown woollen tunics and tied a belt around the waist. Enough of the cloth overlapped to cover their body.

As they walked up the paths trodden by countless feet over the years, they came upon a patch of blackberries and bushes with sloe berries on them.

They picked and ate the blackberries and decided to collect more after they returned to cook and eat.

As they continued picking the berries and eating them, for they were hungry, a man came down the path and stopped.

He stood watching them. Finally, he called out to the men, "Be thee monks?"

The men looked at him, then at each other. One then came closer to the man questioning them.

"Indeed, we are Sir," He turned to the youngest of the men and said, "He is brother Aaron and turning to the other said, and this be brother Clement. I am brother Edmond."

"Well good fellows," said the man, "if you are hungry, then come to my house and share our bounty, for none shall starve while I can fill their belly."

Edmond smiled and turned to his brothers who smiled back at him but said nothing.

Turning again to the man he said, "It will be a pleasure to share your food brother, god moves in mysterious ways, but seems to always provide through others helping hand."

They followed the man to his house, which was rather large and was the farmers home.

The farmer bid them to enter his home, and they were told to sit at the table and his wife would soon add three more places.

Soon they were eating a meat stew with the farmer and the family seemed happy to have them joining them for the meal.

At the end of the meal, they were asked to

drink a jug of ale with the farmer.

As the farmer poured the ale into cups, he asked, "Why have you not shaved your heads like the other monks that passed through here have done?"

"We have only just finished our training and now started to build a retreat for our sleeping. Now our wanderings have brought us here, and we have started to build a sanctuary to welcome all. Once we are happy that we have succeeded in that quest, then we will shave our heads and make cowls to cover it when we walk among the poor."

The farmer nodded as if he understood, but as Edmund had only just made this up, how could he?

They made small talk as they drank, then begged their leave from the farmer thanking him for the meal.

Once in the open they returned back to their retreat or sanctuary, and once inside the dwelling, the sat and then the eldest started talking.

"We must now decide what's to do."

"Well, that was a shock, and a surprise. We ones, common as muck, mistaken for monks. And a slapping good meal with meat to boot," said Clement.

"If we are to stay, then we must make ourselves look the part," said Aaron.

"Agreed," said Edmund, "but no one must catch us out."

They talked for a while longer, then Edmund asked, "Do we have any other woollen cloth that we can make rough cowls out of to go with our habit?"

The others laughed.

Clement and Aaron searched through the bags and found some oddments that they kept for repairs to their clothes.

Pulling out some fine twine from a roll they had pilfered in the last town they passed through, the brothers sat and made three cowls.

A small band of red was cut up and sewn on their cloak in the shape of a cross over the heart.

The three were indeed brothers, and Aaron was the youngest, Clement the next and Edmund was the eldest.

But holy they were not.

Holy terrors were the closest they got to that word. They were rouges, who took advantage of the good, relieved many a maiden of her virtue through lies and deceit, and stole as much as they could to barter with as they travelled though the country.

They had only just crossed into the boarder of Somerset escaping the local Sheriff after he found his wife entertaining one of the brothers.

Truth to say, they were good looking lads, but Jack the lads, should always make sure that the husband doesn't come back a little earlier than expected. Clement had time to grab his cloak and jump out of the window, and as he described it, "Run bare assed naked through the town displaying all his wares to the townsfolk."

The brothers now started to cut the others hair, and once a circle had been chopped, then the knife came out, used to skin and bone an animal.

The top of his head was made wet, then the brother drew with care, the blade across the top of the head, until nothing was showing, other than the ring of hair around the bald patch.

"This had better be worth it, brother," said Clement as he changed places with Aaron.

"What I don't understand is why the fools cut their hair off, then wear a hood to keep the top warm."

Clement shaved Edmund's head and soon they all agreed that they looked more like monks.

"Right brothers, we are truly brothers, but now we are brothers doing God's work. That doesn't mean you change the local virgins thoughts on chastity brother Aaron and brother Clement. This is how we must address ourselves from now on."

"But Edmund, what if we are asked to say something religious?"

"Remember brother Thomas who came to our village. He would greet people with words like, 'Blessings be upon you,' or 'Go with God.' We can do the same."

They settled down for the night and slept well.

The following morning, while Clement and Aaron did what Edmund had asked them to do, Edmund walked up to the village called Winterbourne.

People were surprised to see a monk moving among them, and some asked what order he was from.

Edmund replied, "There are three of us, and we are from the order of the sacred cross," pointing to the red cross over his heart.

He walked to the smithy's and sorted out some pots and pans. He then asked for a special order, and could he wait?

Edmund left the smith to make his special order and wandered around the village looking at the things on offer to buy.

After an idle hour, passing out a few 'God be with you,' comments, he returned to the smiths and found his order finished.

Can you loan me a small hand cart to take all of these things down to our sanctuary? I will return it tomorrow."

They said they did have a small hand cart, and if they couldn't trust a monk, who could they trust?

Edmund smiled; this dodge was going to make things so much easier. After all, monks were basically honest, weren't they?

They even loaded the things into the cart and put a few carrots and potatoes in as a gift to Gods helpers.

Edmund drew his purse out and paid for the items, then pulled the cart out from the smithy's yard.

He pulled it down the hilly track to the new dwelling and on his arrival his brothers showed him the work they had done.

"We now need to hide the entrance," he said, "the thicket will prevent most who might become inquisitive. But to be sure, it must be hidden."

They worked on this and once satisfied, returned to their dwelling, and made a rough table of wood. The two brothers had felled a small tree, cut it in two the long way through the trunk. This formed the tabletop. They used a cross shape to become the legs then once completed they put the table at an angle in part of the room.

Now Edmund placed the special order on the rough table in the centre. The brothers looked at it and then Aaron said, "Do you think it is good enough to fool anyone who comes here."

"It is a plain cross, for three lowly monks. No one will expect more," said Edmund.

He continued, "We now have two cook pots, tomorrow we will dine well. It will mean one of us must find where we can use our skills, and as Aaron is the best man with a bow, then I think he should go."

Aaron nodded and pulled out his hunting knife and took a small pack with him and left his brothers.

The two remaining brothers worked until sundown and soon both were happy that the secret place was well hidden. They now had one cook pot on show.

They ate some bread and some cheese and sat talking about the plans to stir up the community. They slowly became tired and so went to bed.

Rising in the morning, they washed then put fresh water into the cookpot and using flint stones, lit a fire under it. The kindling soon caught and the built the fire up and put the scrap wood onto the fire and soon had a good blaze going. Edmund then said, "Wash the potatoes and carrots, chop up then both and put it into the pot. I am going to return the cart as promised, and we may get some more donations on my way.

Edmund left his brother and pulled the cart up the hill to the village.

As he arrived, so did six soldiers, mounted on horses.

They looked over the monk then called everyone to gather near.

When most had come near, one shouted, "We have found a slaughtered deer in the forest. This is a crime against the King. Have any of you any knowledge of this or been offered meat from the Kings deer."

Everyone shook their heads including the monk.

"It is a crime punishable by death and if I catch any one of you doing this, or eating the flesh of a deer, I shall make sure that it will be a slow death."

The man then nodded to the rest of his troop and rode away.

Having returned the cart, Edmund started to walk down the track to the dwelling, carrying some sacks that had been offered to him.

On arrival, he found that Aaron had arrived back from his nightly outing, and they sat for a while and talked about the meat that they would be going to get once the hue and cry settled down.

Edmund became aware of the sounds of horses coming, and said to his brothers, "Quickly, into the sanctuary, onto your knees in front of the table and then bow your head with hands flat, looking as if we are praying."

They went inside quickly, sank to their knees and then in a line in front of the crude table, took up the pose of three praying monks.

Edmund began to chant, it was nonsense but then, it was what the guests would expect of monks.

A soldier looked in, then went back to his leader. They heard him say "Three monks praying."

"Get them out here now," they heard the leader command.

The soldier returned and in a loud voice said, "My lord commands that you come from this hovel and stand before him."

Edmund stood, then said, "Come brothers, for we are required to meet a new master."

They came from the sanctuary and stood in a line before the horse's and men riding them.

"Who are you, and why are you here?"

"We are the brothers of the sacred cross. We came here two days ago and put down our holy cross on this common land."

"Yet you do not bow to me, acknowledging that I am your Lord."

"No, Sir. We do not. I acknowledge that you are indeed a noble Lord, but we bow only to one Lord, and he is above even an exalted man such as yourself."

"Have a care monk. I could have you all

flogged for your ill manners."

"Indeed, you could Sir, but when the King gets this news and hears about the fogging of his disciples wearing the crusading sacred cross, that even his knights have on their shields, he will not be best pleased.

The Lord looked troubled then said, "Very well monk, I shall overlook this, but think on this. Should you hear of anyone killing a Kings deer, tell us and you will be rewarded."

"I was in the village of Winterbourne when returning a cart and heard that a deer had been killed in the Kings wood. I also saw the soldiers inspecting the cooking pots of the villagers."

"Yes, nothing was found. Slaughtered pig, bits of butchered beef sold in the market, and fowl, but no venison to prove they had done wrong."

"Then good Sir, if we may have the carcass of the deer, to stew the bones for our selves and the poor who may come here for sustenance, you would be aiding Gods work."

"Better you remove it, than vermin come crawling in."

He pointed to a soldier and said, You, stay with the monks, and when they are ready, guide them to the carcass. If you see any strangers, stop them and search them."

"Yes, my Lord."

The soldier dismounted and tied his horse to a tree.

He walked to the cooking pot.

"What have you in here, we did not check your meal."

The soldier was a lot cleverer than his master.

He had recognised that they were, indeed, strangers.

"We have potatoes, carrots, some cabbage and some herbs in it."

"We would welcome some bones to add some flavour, so the deer will be a blessing to add to our pot."

Then the sooner you are ready, the sooner we can collect it."

"Is it far," asked Clement.

"A few miles, you will need to move, for my horse will not hang around waiting for you."

The brothers pulled out a few sacks that had been given to them and walked by the soldier's horse.

The soldier kicked the horse into a faster pace, and the brothers started to jog along to keep up with him.

Laughing, the soldier increased the pace yet again, and the were now running behind the horse that was rapidly leaving them.

As the soldier disappeared around a bend, the brothers slowed and Aaron said, "Quickly, this way," and cut through the trees at his side.

They followed a small track and came out onto the path that the soldier was waiting on.

Seeing them arrive, he spurred the horse again, and the monks broke into another run to keep up.

The game finally ended when the soldier pulled up and got down from his horse.

"It's here behind this tree. My job is done, now I leave you to clear up this mess and return to your temporary dwelling."

He mounted his horse again and turned the horse and rode back the way they had come.

After he had gone, the brothers cut up some bones, and then walked deeper into the wood.

They scraped out a wide and somewhat deep hole then dragged the rest of the deer carcass into the grave they had made.

Breaking the animal up, they soon had it in the hole and scrapped the soil over it.

They picked up a few stones and put that over it, then dragged leaves and other forest litter over it.

Returning to the path, they lifted their bags with a few bones in it, and walked back to their home.

Aaron could have guided them to the deer, but then the soldier would have known who had killed the deer.

Once in their sanctuary, they washed the bones, put them into the pot with the vegetables in, then went to their secret area, and lifted the thorns and bracken to reveal another small area with the second cooking pot.

Aaron had put meat into this before he joined the brothers, and a low fire was cooking the meat nice and slowly. Hanging on twigs all around were large strips of red flesh, hanging to dry.

Aaron poked into the pot, a long metal rod with a point on it, and out came a big chunk of deer meat. He dropped this into a large wooden bowl and pulled out yet another chunk.

The brothers sat and ate the meat, each lifting

a chunk into a small bowl that was his own.
They were tearing strips from the chunks with
their fingers, enjoying the flavour of the slow
cooked meat and wiping the juice's away with
their sleeves.

When they had eaten enough, then damped
the fire, and covered the pot.

Returning to the sanctuary, they pulled out
some vegetables and they sat eating the small
amount in their bowls putting a bone on the
plate once finished.

"Well brothers, we ate like a King this
evening, and with the dried meat, we shall do
so again."

They all agreed and leaving the bones in a
pile near the fire, they washed their small bowls
and the bigger one. This was returned to the
second pot area.

They slept well and the following morning,
they agreed that a little walk would help with
their next plan.

The brothers made their way up to the
village, then turned and started walking along
a wide track the local people called the High
street and came to the Lords home.

In front of them was a high wall and this
seemed to be all the way around.

It would take some effort to climb over, but
not impossible. A pond was behind them and
as the watched, a servant come from a small
doorway with food waste, and then dump it by
the pond.

Dogs came from around the area, and it was
soon spread all over the place.

The brothers turned the corner following the wall, noting where the building was that was inside the walls.

Eventually, they had walked around the whole of the wall, and although the big archway around the corner from the pond was the obvious way in, the brothers had no intention of using that.

They returned to their sanctuary and decided to watch the side door once again the next day.

Over the next few days, the watched the servant bring out the food rubbish and drop it onto the rise in front of the pond.

It was a reasonably regular event.

That evening, they decided that tomorrow was the time for the plan to take place.

They worked out how it should happen, and once sorted in their mind, they settled down for a sleep, all but Aaron. He took his hunting knife and left the brothers as it grew dark.

When the brothers woke, Aaron was back, confirming that a new kill could be found.

The brothers had a quick bite to eat and Aaron showed them where the kill was.

All returned and waited the morning out, As the afternoon was drawing to a close, the three brothers went up into the village, and passed through on the way to the pond, without anyone seeing them.

Two brothers waited outside but near the small doorway.

Aaron went running around the corner of the wall towards the gateway of the Mount, the Lord and Ladies house behind the wall, shouting as loud as he could.

As he got to the gateway, a guard stopped him and he pretended he was out of breath as he told them that another deer had been killed and his brother was trying to follow the rouges who did it as the move down towards the Severn sea that divides Wales from England.

"Can you show us where it is?" asked the guard as he waved others to him.

"Yes, but I have run all the way here, and am in need of a rest first before I run back."

"Tell his Lordship, he will want to know." said the sergeant in charge.

With men dashing around, the servant opened the side door and as he stepped out, a monk ran up to him and put his arms around him, saying, "Has my brother arrived? I couldn't run as fast as he."

"I don't know monk, but there is a commotion within these wall's."

"Ah. Then it sounds as if he has arrived, thank you friend," and he let the man go to rid himself of the food waste.

Clement staggered away acting exhausted and the servant threw the slops away and returned to the gate. He then passed through and locked the door with the key.

He hung it on a hook near the door and walked through the trees and shrubs towards the house.

Edmund watched him go, then unhooked the key and opened the door, and Clement slipped through.

Once in, he pushed it shut, but put a small

stone in front of it, to stop it opening by itself.

They made their way through the trees and shrubbery, and then once they were on the opposite side to the troops , they stripped their monks habit from their bodies, and stood with the new clothes they wore underneath.

They were now wearing a once white smock top, and baggy trousers, that was black with stains from the charcoal that had been boiled with it.

The last piece of disguise was a hood that covered their head, but had a circle cut in it for them to look through.

Both brothers started to climb up the building, and with ivy growing on it, it was not hard.

They reached the big window that was their target, and pushed it further open and climbed in.

They were in a bedroom, and each pulled out a sack from the baggy trousers and started to put anything they found of value into them.

Candle sticks of silver, a ring, anything they saw went into the bags.

Next, they left the bedroom and crept along the corridor to another room.

This looked as if it was the Lords room, for here they found a chest at the bottom of the bed, and the key was still in it.

Opening it up, they found gold coins belts with stones in it that shone and could be diamonds.

The chest was emptied.

Both bags were now extremely heavy, and it

was decided that enough was enough.

They returned to the bedroom, and one brother climbed down and waited as the other tied each bag and lowered it down. He then followed the bags down. They coiled the rope, then made their way round towards the small door, and once there, opened it slowly to check no one was near.

Abandoning the hoods, they pulled a dark floppy hat over their head, and then left by the door and went along the other side of the pond. They made their way down the hill towards the lower part of the road to Bristol, keeping an eye out for anyone walking through the woods the same way.

A brief stop was made to change into the monks habit, and with the cowl down and the hat in the pockets of the disguise under the habit they continued on the circuitous route.

They crossed the lower Bristol road and avoided the hamlet of Barton.

Crossing Bradley brook, they started to change direction towards their sanctuary, and eventually arrived there.

They took the animal skin they had saved from the deer and piled all of the stolen things into the middle.

Next, they collected a pole, that was left ready for the job, and putting in through the cooking pot, they lifted it from the fire. They next drew the fire to one side and exposed a metal pot as they pulled the soil away.

They lifted the lid, then both raised the skin with their purloined items, and stuffed it into the pot.

Edmund replaced the lid, then put the ashes and the small burning fire over it.

Both then lifted the cooking pot and replaced it over the fire, once again hanging on the wooden pole across the fire.

They threw a small amount of sticks on the fire and were pleased to see that it started to burn. Both now turned and ran into the woods and dashed along animal trails until they could hear shouting and calling in front of them.

Taking care to avoid the men searching, they passed them and then came out ahead of them.

Edmund said to Clement, "Sorry brother," and punched him hard in the face, then as he fell, saved him but smeared the blood from his lip onto his face.

He called loudly and was pleased to find that within a few moments, the horses arrived to find him nursing his brother and bits of blood on his face.

"What happened? Have they got away?"

"We were following them, but others came to help carry the meat that was in bags over their shoulders."

He looked up at the Lord he had robbed and said in a sad voice, "They beat us and told us not to follow them."

"Which way did they go?" asked the Lord.

"This path, they took that but then seemed by their voices to go off the track somewhere over that way. There must now be six or seven of them."

"We have a chance to catch them men thanks

to these brave monks, now split up and search for them," shouted the Lord, "a barrel of ale for the man who sees the first one. Monk, stay and help your brother back to your dwelling. Bring back the horse tomorrow."

They rode on leaving Aaron now with his brothers.

Once they were gone, Clement said, "You punch hard for a holy man."

They put Clement on the horse and made their way back to the dwelling.

They had been back for quite a while, the cooking pot bubbling away nicely.

The Lord arrived and as he stopped, a soldier jumped from his horse and held the reigns.

"Well monks, I cannot say I welcomed you here, but you have proved a valuable help to our care intrusted on us by the King to watch over his chase. I wish to reward you all and if you will come to the Mount, my home in the village, I will give you some coins each for your troubles and help."

Edmund stood and said, "Good Sir. We need no reward for stopping those who would break Gods commandments. Steal not from your fellow man, least God smites the hand that steals."

"Yes, well. Then accept a barrel of ale from me, to sup after your meal."

"We will accept this gift good Sir if it would please you. Did you catch the rogues that killed the deer Sir?"

"No, they got away, but one day soon, mark my words."

The lord told the soldier to mount up, and they took the horse that Aaron had rode on.

"We thank you Sir, blessings be upon you."

They rode away and once the horses had gone and no sound could be heard, Edmund said, "He came back to collect the horse in case we cooked it and ate it."

They all laughed.

The following morning, a soldier on horseback with another horse with a barrel of ale strapped on it arrived.

He got down from his horse and took the barrel from the other horse.

Setting it down, he turned and said, "The Lord is raging around the Mount this morning."

"What has been the cause of this then, I hope tis not a bad tooth."

"Worse than that. A thief broke into the Mount and stole valuables from him. No one knows who did this, but he is in a foul mood. Still he remembered his word to thee. This is the ale he said he would give you. I must be on my way now, for I was told to return in haste."

He mounted his horse and rode away.

The brothers grinned at each other.

Over the next week, the brothers broke up the hoard, packed it into the skin again and buried most of it in a pot in a hole near the pool next to their sanctuary. They then abandoned the building and left their treasure behind to collect in the future. They left knowing that the pots and pans for cooking they couldn't take would be taken by any who followed.

Over the years, others made use of the pole house, but it slowly fell to pieces.

The brothers never returned for their treasure, for eight months after they left, they were hanged when they were caught stealing from a Lord in the region they next went to.

The Lord in Winterbourne never recovered his items, this was still was buried near the pool and the monks sanctuary. The Lord had found the servants door open and knew how the thieves had got in to steel from him. As a result, he then had the doorway bricked up.

If you look at the wall when next you are at the pond in Winterbourne, you will see the bricked-up entrance.

And that is why to this day, their sanctuary area is known as Monks pool.

Authors note

This is a story, so please don't get your metal detector and go down searching for the treasure.

Billy's Pond

There are a lot of tales about Billy's Pond and this is just another.

I have lived in a village called Winterbourne and have done so for the last fifty odd years.

I have passed the area that is fenced off many times and heard the comments that the pool is bottomless.

If it is, then it will never give up its secrets.

What I am about to tell you is a shocking consequence of an accident, and how this became known as Billy's pond.

For the sake of this tale we need to go quite a way back in time, to the period when in 1402 King Richard the second was on the throne.

He had just granted to the Lord Edmund Bradlington and the Lady Blanche Bradlington the rights to govern over the lands of Gloucestershire and Somersetshire. They also had the rights to allow the village of Winterbourne and Chipping Sodbury under their jurisdiction, to hold markets and fairs on given days.

The Lord and Lady chose to reside in the castle of Brygstow.

The Lord ruled on behalf of the King and Sheriffs were appointed to see justice was upheld on their behalf.

At the time of our tale, there was a lad known as Willie who lived in the village of Winterbourne.

He was a strong and handsome lad and offered his hand to any labour that was needed to keep his head and that of his mother's above water.

It was a hard life for the lower order but when the local Sheriff suggested that he should do work for him, he jumped at the chance.

Willie's job wasn't arduous, nor was it an auspicious job, but it gave him a regular small amount of money as an income, and any food left over from the table of the Sheriff and his soldiers.

He would arrive at the Sheriff's house each morning as the sun rose, and start to muck out the stalls that the horses were in.

Willie washed down the stables, fed the horses and watered them.

He would clean the silver bridle on the horse's reigns which the Sheriff rode, and oil the leather straps and saddles.

Nothing was too much of a problem for him.

When the sheriff shouted for his stool to come so that he might mount his horse, Willie ran to his master and on hands and knee, let the Sheriff use his back for a stool.

Behind his back, the soldiers ridiculed Willie, and called him names that although were meant to offend, had no impact on the young man's bearing.

On one occasion, the men pushed the wheel barrow over full of horse droppings, and kicked it all over the place, but Willie just got a broom, swept it up, and put it back into the barrow, then wheeled it away.

Eventually, they gave up their sport.

It was after about six months, when the Spring was beginning to show, that thee Lord and Lady Bradlington and their daughter came to Winterbourne on a judicial visit.

The Sheriff collected taxes from the people, and the amounts needed to be checked.

The daughter of the Lord, Mistress Edith Bradlington had also come with them, and once her parents had settled in the Sheriff's house, she wandered down to the stables.

There she chanced upon Willie who was grooming one of the horse's and talking to it.

She watched him quietly at first, then spoke to him.

"Are you any relation to my Lord Sheriff?"

Willie turned and looked at the vision before him.

She was truly a higher class than he, and he bowed his head to acknowledge this.

"If it does please thee Mistress, I am but a labourer, but I handle the horse's and mucks them out."

"What is your name pray."

"I be known as Willie, Mistress."

"Well Willie, saddle up a horse for me to ride, and I shall go forth and see what this place has to offer me."

"But Mistress, tis the Sheriff's horses and I cannot do so without his orders."

"Do you ride Willie?"

"I do Mistress, but only to see if a horse be better after I have rubbed his legs down after a hard ride."

"Very well. Stay here and I will see what the Sheriff has to say."

Willie stayed by the horse, and after a short wait, The Sheriff, Lord Bradlington and Mistress Edith came to the stables.

The Lord said, "It is my daughters wish to ride out into the country and she has stated that you refused to grant her that wish."

"I cannot tell a lie my Lord, tis true."

"Then she can go on her ride, but with you at her side as a guide, but daughter, do not fail me. If this fellow tells you that it would not be safe to ride somewhere, then bow to his knowledge. If you fail to do as he says, and trouble ensues, I will not flog you, but I will flog him."

At this, Willie shuddered.

"Yes father," she said.

Lord Bradlington then turned to Willie and pointed a finger at him.

"You hear me well. If a single hair of my daughter is hurt, I will skin you alive. Make sure you take heed of this warning. She must remain virtuous and untouched, for her coming marriage."

Willie shuddered again at the thought. What had he got himself into now?

They left Mistress Edith and returned to the house.

As Willie saddled the two horses up, one with a side saddle, two guards came out of the guard quarters with the sergeant of arms.

These were some men who had escorted the entourage to the Sheriff's house.

"Saddle up two more horses, these men will

be going with you Mistress Edith, on the Lords express orders. The guide will lead, the guards will follow."

Willie did as he was told, and everyone stood and watched as he completed his task.

Mistress Edith then went to mount her horse, but no stool was available.

When the guards ask Willie where it was kept, he said, "I am it."

He went to the horse, bent down on hands and knees and the lady with the help of the stool stepped up, turned, and then sat on the horse. She adjusted her leg and Willie then stood and went back to the horses.

Everyone now mounted and Willie led them out onto the High street and turned towards Chipping Sodbury. They rode for a short way, then turned down a track towards the hamlet of Yonder.

The mistress Edith was not happy with the ride and rode up to be beside her guide.

"This is no excitement, can we not cut across the country and ride fast."

"Better we don't Mistress. The place is full of ruts and if you fell, then it would be my hide, not thine that feels the pain."

She looked back at the two guards who had closed up to them both and she shouted, "Follow me."

Edith spurred the horse into a fast gallop and as she passed Willie so did the guards who were taken by surprise.

Willie chased after them as she raced up the fields and then on reaching the lane going towards Winterbourne, she rode into a stand of trees that grew next to the Mount.

When Willie got to the trees, he was shocked to see that Mistress Edith was on the ground and the two guards were stood looking at her.

Willie moved closer to her, and bent down to her side,

Blood was coming from her forehead, and she was lying very still.

Willie rose and opening his shirt, tore a piece from it. He walked to the pool and wet the cloth then returned to the girl.

He lifted her head with one hand and wiped her forehead softly to clean the wound.

One of the guards came to Willie and said, "Unhand her varlet. The Mistress should not be touched by such as you. The Lord has her promised by marriage to Sir Richard Glancey, and he will not receive a bride sullied by a yokels hand."

As this was being said, Edith had opened her eyes and looked up at the young man who was looking after her cut.

She felt a strange feeling come over her, as she looked at him, her head still cradled in his hand.

Then he looked down at her. Hazel eyes met blue eyes, and Willie smiled at her.

"Tis good to see Mistress that the blow did not do thee much damage, but now, if you can, it would be good to rise, and return thee to your father, for I fear, he will be full of anger for this accident that has befallen upon us both."

He lifted her into a sitting position, then

offered his hand to assist her to stand.

She took it and she stood, then he led her to the horse, got on all fours and she climbed up onto the horse with the help of the guards, who were wearing gloves.

Willie got back on his horse and they made their way to the Sheriffs house.

Mistress Edith was helped down, and Willie was told to wait in the stables. One of the guards stood next to the stall he was in, barring his way out.

Willie waited for a while wondering about his fate. It had not been his fault, but he had been charged to look after Mistress Edith and had failed.

After a while, Lord Bradlington arrived with the other guard and the Sheriff. There was no sign of Mistress Edith.

"I have heard the sorry tale, and I rue the day I entrusted my daughters safety in your hands."

"My Lord, I…"

"Silence," shouted the Lord.

The next comment came from the Sheriff.

"You are my man, and it is my duty to punish you on two counts. You did not look after your charge of keeping Mistress Edith safe, and you did assault her body as she laid helpless in a swoon."

"But Sheriff, I…"

"Silence," demanded the Sheriff.

Willie stopped and looked at both of the men.

Then Lord Bradlington said, "Call four of your men Sheriff, hardy sorts who will enjoy punishing this creature, for I do not want him standing and looking at me."

The Sheriff called the Master of the arms, and told him what he needed, and the man ran to the garrison to pick four men.

When those who were chosen, arrived, they were told to take off their tunics and prepare to teach this varlet a lesson.

They quickly did as they were told, grins all over their faces as they advanced on Willie.

One grabbed his arm as another punched him in the stomach.

They then came at him from all sides, beating him, twisting his limbs, and pounding him to a bloody mess. He didn't stand a chance.

Each time he fell, he was hoisted up, and hit again. Then they kicked him.

When at last he made no movement to resist, the Lord who had watched with the Sheriff, and saw this justice being served said, "Now take this thing out of my sight and leave him at the scene of the crime. Break the hand that touched my daughter."

"It was both hands my Lord," said one of the guards who had been there.

"Then both shall be broken to end it."

They lifted the shattered body of Willie and hung him over the horse.

The two guards and one of the Sheriff's men rode out and went along the High street, then through the village.

The people watched the soldiers pass and saw the body of Willie, or Billy as they called him, draped across the horse.

Eventually they arrived at the stand of trees with the pool in it.

They all stopped near the pool and they pulled Willie's body from the horse allowing it to drop to the ground with a thud.

Willie gave a groan as he landed but could barely see out of either eye.

The Sheriffs soldier, went into the trees, found a fallen branch, and pulled it to Willie still laying where he had dropped.

He lifted Willie's arm onto the branch and lifted his boot. He then stamped down onto the arm and the snap was clearly heard as Willie rolled towards the broken arm reaching out to the sudden pain and screaming at the agony of the break.

The Sheriff's man showed no emotion as he took hold of Willie's hair.

He then dragged him round so that the other side of Willie's body was nearest to the branch. He took his other arm and placed it on the branch.

Again, the noise of the break was drowned out by the scream from Willie.

The Sheriff's soldier now walked back to his horse and said, "You are my witness. Justice was served, as his Lordship decreed."

Both nodded, and they left Willie to his agony.

On their return, the three men were ushered into the room that that Sheriff and Lord Bradlington were seated in.

Sat in another chair, looking crestfallen, was Edith.

"Well, is it done?"

"Yes, my Lord," said the Sheriff's man, "By my own boot did I break both arms as you declared must be done."

He nodded and turned to his daughter. "You see daughter, a lesson to any serf who dares to touch you. You can be sure that this will never happen again, when the word gets out."

"But father, I told you, it was I that rode away from the guards and the guide, and it was I that hit a low branch through my own foolishness."

"Nonsense, Edith, I shall hear no more of it. Now go to your room and divest thyself of your clothes and go to bed. Justice has been served."

Edith left the room but did not go to her bedroom.

She slipped down some side stairs and out into the courtyard.

Horses were still saddled and waiting in the stalls to be dealt with.

She quietly went into a stall and moved the horse in it to the side. The stall had bars running longways and she used this as a ladder to climb on the horse.

The wilful girl then kicked the horse into motion and shot out of the stall. She expertly turned the horse and rode through the gateway much to the amazement of the guard who stood there.

She rode down the High street and into the Village and soon arrived at the pond where Willie was lying.

Edith dropped from the horse and went to Willie, his body twisted and misshaped from his mistreatment.

She went to the pond and then tore some of her undergarments in strips and wetting them, returned to Willie.

Washing his face and cleaning his eyes, she saw that one eye showed a glimpse of the hazel she had seen.

"Rest easy, for you do not deserve this, and I will try my best to right the wrong my father and the Sheriff has done to you."

Willie stirred, and then she heard the sound of horses coming to where they were.

"Quickly," she said, "Let me help you up, and I will try to hide you."

She pulled at his arm, and he cried out, so she put her head under the arm at the armpit and lifted as he slowly stood on shaky legs.

The noise of horse and shouts of the pursuers was now loud, and she pulled him deeper into the trees and nearer to the pool.

As she reached the pool, she dropped Willie, and he screamed, and the men rushed towards the sound.

She was bending down pulling at Willie when they broke into the small open area and saw what she was doing.

"Leave him Mistress, your father has sent us to find you and bring you back."

She stood up, her back to the pool, and said, "I will tend to this man who has been sorely treated, then I will return, but only then."

The Sheriff's man moved closer and the other

two closed on her from the other side.

She moved sideways from the Sheriff's man and tripped on a root at the pools edge.

Edith fell onto Willie, who again screamed in pain and kicked out at the cause.

Edith rolled into the pool and thrashed for a moment as the cold water struck her. Then her clothes soaked up the water and she sank down as the soldiers watched in horror. A stream of bubbles breaking the surface as she descended into the depths.

The guard nearest then said, "She fell on him," pointing to Willie. "We must tell the sad truth that this man took revenge on his Lordship, by killing his daughter who had only come to help him."

"Yes, I saw him kick her. What chance did she have against such as he? He is a big man and couldn't use his arms, so used his powerful legs," said another realising that they had an answer to their problem.

"This was how it happened, but now the swine who committed the crime, should suffer the same fate," said the second guard.

They pushed Willie over and as he screamed in pain, they rolled him into the pool.

Willie sank at once, bubbles coming from his mouth.

They watched for a minute or two, but Willie did not rise, and the bubbles stopped.

They rode back and told their story, and as people got to hear of it, so the rummers of a love tryst came about.

And that dear reader, is my sorry tale of the

pool known as Billy's pool.

Authors note

Brygstow

The change in the form of the name 'Bristol' is due to the local pronunciation of 'ow' as 'ol'. Later the 'g' was dropped and Brystol became the usual pronunciation. The change of spelling came later.

The Governing Lord

The Lord Edmund Bradeston was the Lord who was given the rights to govern over the lands of Gloucestershire and Somersetshire for the King. Lady Blanche Bradeston was his wife who also was the recipient for the rights for allowing markets and fairs in the regions within their control.
(A history of Winterbourne. H W N Ludwell)

For the sake of this story, I have changed the name of Lord Bradeston to Lord Bradlington. I have no intention to besmirch the surname of the man or indeed his descendants.

The Dram Way

My wife and I like walking, and on this occasion, we drove out to Bitterwell Lake. We walked around the lake and then found the walkway for the dram way.

Although I had heard of it, I had not delved into its history.

Once home, I found information about it and this story, started to build in my mind.

Mines were being sunk on the Heath, later to be called, Coalpit Heath.

The owners of the mines needed to get the coal to Bristol as quickly as they could, and the dram way was built for that purpose.

Jeremiah Tynsdale heard about the need for owners with their own strong horses to apply for work pulling wagons from the pit heads down a railway track, to the river, where they would load the coal onto barges waiting to take the coal down river into Bristol.

Jeremiah and his horse, Gypsy had been pulling barges along the canals from Gloucester to Sharpness near Bristol.

From there, the barge would be taken by other means onto the River Severn down to Bristol.

He had been walking the sixteen miles backwards and forwards for quite an age when word reached his ear about a new kind of job for his cart horse and himself.

The more he thought about it, the more he

felt he needed a change.

His horse and he would need to leave Sharpness and travel down to the place called Coalpit Heath, and then register with one of the pits. Then they would pull the drams from the pit to a loading bay in a place called Keynsham.

Well it didn't sound so bad. It was a wagon on wheels, not like the barges on water, and if Gypsy could pull a heavy loaded barge, he could certainly pull a wagon on wheels.

Having convinced himself, on reaching Sharpness, he collected his pay, and left the yard, and started on his way.

Gypsy would need rests between travelling and sleeping to get there.

Jeremiah arrived two days later at a pithead called Ram Hill.

He was told how the system worked and how he and Gypsy would fit in.

It seemed that four or five drams (wagons) would freewheel down the line with brake men holding the long break handles called spraggs.

Once the drams stopped on the level lands, they were then uncoupled from each other and a horse would pull the dram up the next hill to the top and unhook it from the horses chains. He would then chock it on the slight slope to stop it running away.

When all of the drams were up on the holding line and coupled, the two brakemen would again ride the dram train down the slope to the next level ground that was a holding area.

Jeremiah would only pull the drams of his

contracted owner, who had their name painted on the side of their drams.

When the drams came back empty and rolled into the flat holding area where he would be working in, he would need to couple up three drams and haul them up the hill to the mine to be loaded once again.

There were double tracks in places, and single in others.

Full wagons coming down had a priority and empty drams should not get in there way.

Junctions came from various pit heads and joined the main line to the first level.

A system of whistles and flags told the drivers of returning drams that they needed to get into the nearest passing loop.

Jeremiah took the metal contract coin and clipped it onto the bridle of Gypsy.

Each dram had a number and as he pulled it loaded to the top of the hill and chocked it, the number was recorded, and his pay was per dram pulled up the hill.

Taking Gypsy by his lead, he took the horse down the track side and ended up at a place called Siston, where exchange tracks to hold drams were located. Here, Gypsy was shackled to a dram, and they pulled it up the slope, linked three or four together ready for freewheeling to the next stage.

They then went to the rear of the empty drams, and the horse was shackled facing the drams. The brakes were then released and with Jeremiah on the lead drams brake, the empty drams rolled back down the hill with the horse at the back holding them back, and Jeremiah assisting the decent into one of the holding lines for returns.

Once the track coming from Coalpit Heath was signalled clear, Gypsy and Jeremiah started on their way back up to the mine, pulling three empty drams.

This then became their daily routine.

Of course, there were problems. Vandals who may have had a grudge against a mine owner, released the brakes on drams waiting to go down a hill on the line, and the freewheeling drams crashed over as they went around corners in an uncontrolled speed.

It was on a cold morning that was coming up towards Winter, that the accident transpired for Gypsy and Jeremiah.

A new rake of drams had arrived for them to haul up the hill ready for the next drop down towards the river.

They were part way up the hill, with a fully loaded dram behind them when Jeremiah looked up and saw four empty drams hurtling down the single track towards them.

Before he could do anything, they crashed into Gypsy, and then left the rails rolling over and hitting Jeremiah.

As the dust settled and other drivers and brakemen arrived, it became clear that the horse was dead, but the driver was alive, however his leg was badly slashed.

Jeremiah was lifted and put onto the soft grass to the side, as they started to sort out the crashed drams, and remove the dead horse.

The full dram had been pushed over, so they undid all the chains and cut the leathers from the horse.

They then pulled the horse from the track and once that part of the track was clear, the *Muster man instructed that they return to the dram that was being pulled up the hill and lift it back onto the track.

With a lot of heaving and swearing, the dram was replaced.

They locked the brake and then picked up as much of the coal as could be dealt with and threw it into the dram.

When it was reloaded to the best of their ability, the Muster man signalled that a dram was coming down, and they released the brake and it rolled back down to the holding lines.

Next, they lifted the other drams onto the track, and as each was in position, it was sent on its way down to the empty holding line.

Once the last one arrived at the holding bay, the Muster man signalled that the next horse could start on its way up the hill.

He bent to Gypsy's bridle and unclipped the metal contract coin, thus ending the mine owners contract with Jeremiah.

Giving a glace around, his eyes briefly setting on Jeremiah, he then walked up to the top of the hill to make sure, no other drams were likely to start coming down.

Nothing should stop the delivery of the coal to the river.

Jeremiah knew that Gypsy was dead, but he still wanted to get near his friend and companion for the last six years.

He looked around, found a strong stick, and stood up as best he could, and limped to the horse.

As he sank to the ground to sit by Gypsy's head, a man came over to him and said he had some bandage and a damp cloth to go on the deep gash.

Jeremiah wasn't worried about himself but allowed the man to cut his trousers up to his thigh, exposing the gash.

The man placed the damp cloth on the wound then as it became red with blood, he wrapped the bandage around the leg as tight as he could and then tied it tightly.

Through all this, Jeremiah just stroked Gypsy's head.

"Come on mate, lets get you to a doctor, he can fix you up."

Jeremiah knew that the horse would be cut up, and used by people for meat, and wouldn't allow the man to take him away.

When the man gave up, Jeremiah lay by Gypsy and continued to stroke the muzzle of his friend.

Drams trundled up and down the rail in front of him, but still he sat there.

During the night, one of the drivers returning down the track slowed then braked his load of empty drams.

He approached the horse and the sleeping man who was leaning over the horse he had lost in the accident.

Coming closer, he could see that the man had

his eyes open resting on the horse's head, but he was clearly dead.

The morning came and both man and horse were gone.

Work for the mine owners continued and went on until the pits closed in 1867.

It was reported that the dram way was extremely safe in its working life, and only one mishap occurred when a horse died due to a collision with runaway drams.

No mention was made of any human loss of life, but then, Jeremiah's contract with the mine owner had been terminated when the Muster man had unclipped the metal contract coin from Gypsy's bridle.

Jeremiah's death was nothing to do with the mine owners, but as money was due to him, he did have a church burial in the mine workers cemetery.

Authors note

Although there is no recognised origin of the word 'dram way', it was used locally to describe a narrow railway used for our local coal industry prior to the start of the steam railway.

The independent hauliers provided their own horse traction and contracted to an owner by taking the mine token and clipping it to the bridle of the horse. This was a common thing to be done, both on independent hauliers on barges and on many other jobs requiring a horse

to work under licence. So, with no knowledge
that it a was fact, I placed it in the story to give
it credibility.

Each of the wagons on the dram way held four
tons of coal.

Accidents happened infrequently, though on
at least one occasion it was reported that the
driver failed to apply the brakes and the wagons
over-ran the drivers horse and killed it.
This information is derived in part from an SBL
related webpage, copyright holder unknown.

Muster man*

I invented this man. Clearly some sort of signal
system was used and most likely, someone
would be in charge to co-ordinate the
movement of the drams.
Again, I speculated that the mine owners would
have had someone that would look after their
interests, and I needed someone to be there to
add to the story.
This is a story, based on some facts, and some
imagination, after all, I admit I am old, but not
so old that I can recall any of this!

JP

A Taste of Bliss

I first saw the tower of the mill in Frampton Cotterell, when I visited a church group to give a talk about my travels.

Now, as I am sat thinking and creating stories, I had an idea for one based around the mill there.

This then is the story of the mill owner, one Herbert Grivins.

Herbert was a parsimonious man, totally unwilling to spend money unless it was deemed unavoidable.

Farmers brought their corn or wheat to be ground, and he would be paid to do so.

But Herbert was not satisfied with just being paid to do the job, he also cheated his customers.

As the corn, wheat or barley was ground down, Herbert syphoned off some of the end product, and made an extra profit.

A man called Jasper Quimble called monthly, and took the small bags to Chipping Sodbury market, where he sold it to customers who wanted only a small amount. Half was Herbert's and the other was Jasper's.

He was a make do and mend sort of person, so his millers coat and trousers had patches on it of various colours. It didn't bother him that the people thought he was weird.

Herbert lived on his own and admitted to himself that he would never meet the right sort of future partner, they all seemed to like spending money.

Mr Sprigger told him just a few days ago that he would be glad when someone took his daughter off his hands, she was spending money faster than he could earn it.

That would never do for Herbert.

Not that he didn't like women, he had had one or two encounters when he was younger, but his conclusion then was that girls were, well different.

He had wondered if George Sprigger had been sounding him out for a potential match.

Herbert shuddered as he thought about that. He had a vision of his secret hoard of money flying out of the mill door.

Work came and went, and Herbert continued to syphon off a small bag of the end product. Once the bags were claimed by the farmer, and he had gone, the small bags would be labelled as pure this or that.

It was on one of his days when he had nothing to do, that he went for a walk through the village and by chance, he passed a stone cottage where an attractive young lady was working with her father in the garden, tying up bean sticks.

"Good day to you Mr Grivins, it's a lovely day to be out and about, is it not?"

Herbert stopped, and looked at the man, not sure if he knew him or not.

"It is a nice day indeed, Sir," said Herbert looking puzzled. Should he know him or not?

"You don't know me, but even strangers

should be able to give a free word or two to a passer-by, don't you think?"

Herbert kept looking at the girl as she stretched up to tie the bean sticks while her father was talking.

He turned again to the man and said, "Yes, it is indeed a poor man who cannot spare a word or two to his fellow man."

"Well Sarah, we are finished here, time to let this busy man get on with his walk."

Saying goodbye, they walked up the garden path, and Herbert stood there watching the girl.

He turned and walked back to the mill and then sat in his kitchen, thinking of the encounter.

The following day, a milling job arrived, but all Herbert could think of was the girl from yesterday.

He was so confused that he forgot to put the syphon on, and the farmer got the full milling.

As the sacks were collected, and money exchanged hands, the thrill he got putting the money into his hidden chest, was subdued by the thought of seeing the girl again.

Herbert changed and again walked the same route, and his heart gave a lurch as again he saw her out pegging clothes on the line.

"Good day to you Sarah. I hope the rain stays away to dry these things. I do my own washing, and put it inside the mill at the top, it soon dries there."

"Oh, hello. My father is at work, so I am finishing a few chores."

"So sorry if I startled you. I was just passing by and felt I should say a few words."

"It's fine, I don't get much conversation with other people, since my mother died, I have taken over the jobs in the house."

"Then it's no point in my asking you if you would like to join me in my wanderings around the village."

"If you can wait, then I would be happy to do so."

Herbert could not believe it. He had asked her to join him, and she had said yes.

She joined him at the front of the house after locking the door.

Herbert, ever the gentleman, went to the outside of the pathway and as they walked, so conversation went over their lives to date.

She told him how she had been to school and had to get used to hand-me-downs and repairing clothes rather than buying new. Now she darned her father's socks to save money. This was all music to Herbert's ears.

He told her about the training his father gave him in the mill. Then how his father had died, and he had taken over the mill. His mother, he told her, had perished two years ago, so he lived on his own.

They walked side by side, no holding hands, but somehow, Herbert felt comfortable with her and he thought that she also felt the same.

After the large circular walk, they came back to Sarah's house, and she thanked him, and went to her front door.

Still he could not take his eyes off her.

She opened the door, stepped in and as she went to close it, he said, "Would you like to look around the mill sometime in the future?"

She paused, then said, "Yes, I would like that."

As she shut the door, Herbert's heart went into overdrive.

He returned to the mill and looked at the flour dust all over the living space.

This would never do.

Then he stopped.

What was happening to him?

He sank into a chair and gave thought to the unspoken question.

It was the girl Sarah. He was smitten by her. But why? He had everything he wanted here.

The more he thought about it, the more he had to accept it, it was more than a fascination, he wanted Sarah to be part of his life.

Herbert had overheard some folks say that when the right one comes along; it can knock you sideways. Sarah had done this to him.

He began to sweep up the dust from the mill and clear the smears of flour from the meagre furniture.

Looking around at the place now, it certainly was an improvement.

That night Herbert had an uncomfortable dream, and on waking, had to go to his hiding place to open the box with his hoard of money.

Nothing had changed, but it had been an unsettling dream.

A small job arrived to mill some corn for winter feed, and as Herbert didn't syphon any of this, the farmer went away with the full load.

Herbert sat drinking a cup of tea when he

heard someone call out to him.

He put the tea down and opened the door.

Standing there was Sarah and her father.

"Sarah was very keen to see your mill, and I would appreciate it if you could bring her back once she has had a look around."

Herbert asked her to step in after her assured her father that he would bring her back.

Sarah was smiling as he came into the room, and when she pointed to his coat and trousers patched by himself, he understood.

"I do my own repairs; I like to save money by doing small jobs of repair like this."

"Any wife would be ashamed to allow her man to go around like that. Oh, sorry, that was very forward of me."

"No. That is fine. I quite understand. Now would you like a cup of tea or take a look around first?"

"Show me around please, and then maybe, we can sit and have a cup of tea after."

He showed her how the grain comes into the mill, how the windmill winds the bags up to the top and then how it drops down slowly grinding the grain and falling into the sacks.

At the top, he showed her his clothesline, and she could see how it would soon dry. It was quite breezy up there.

He told her to be careful coming down and he went first to catch her should she fall.

Once back down in the living room, she asked, "Were do you sleep?"

He got up from the seat and showed her the door behind the kitchen area. This led to an extension to the brick walls of the windmill.

It wasn't much, but then when you close your eyes, what did it matter?

She sat on the bed and then lay back.

"Well, its a nice soft bed," she said, and then sat up again.

She then said, "Herbert, are we courting?"

Herbert was taken aback by the question, but gathering his thoughts, said, "I believe we are. Look, this is all new to me, and to be honest with you, I have had nothing to do with young ladies before this. But Sarah, I hope that these strange feelings I have for you are matched for me."

"Indeed, they are Herbert. I couldn't sleep very well last night. I kept thinking about you and I as..."

"Husband and wife," finished Herbert.

"Oh yes, you feel it also."

He moved over to her, and she suddenly stood, threw her arms around his neck, and kissed him slowly rubbing herself against him. This caused Herbert an acute problem that he did his best to stop her being aware of.

She stepped back, grinned at him and said, "Would you like to meet me tomorrow, about this sort of time? Father can bring me up here if it's okay with you."

Herbert couldn't think of anything he would like better.

He walked her home and then had another restless night.

No work came in the following day, and he changed his work clothes and waited for Sarah to come.

As their romance blossomed so the inevitable question came up.

When are we going to get married?

Herbert, Sarah, and Joe, talked through the proposed wedding, but Sarah asked if it could be a quiet wedding, this would save money and speed things up.

Herbert's heart went out to his future wife, she was of a like mind as he was.

The wedding day came, and Sarah wore her mother's bridal dress, to save money she said.

Once they registrar said they were man and wife, they returned back to the mill, where all three had a cold meal and a drink of tea.

As Sarah's father left them, he said to her, "Be happy."

Sarah didn't seem shy about undressing in front, of him, but Herbert tried his best to cover the embarrassing bits.

Sarah laughed and came around to his side of the bed. She took his hands away from his lower body, smiled and said, "Now, hurry up and get into bed husband, I want this marriage consummated, and you are primed and ready."

Still not sure that he should be totally naked, he cleared the last bits of his dress and got into the bed with his wife.

The night was as far as Herbert was concerned, something that was unbelievably good.

Sarah exhausted him.

He woke in the morning to find her with her arms around him, and the bedclothes at the bottom of the bed.

The routine work of running a mill went on, with Sarah hooking the grain bags up and sending it up for Herbert to unhook and pour the contents down the chute to be ground.

She was a willing worker, and always checked the payment was correct. She then placed it into a small box and put it in the living room on the small table.

Herbert went on syphoning the small amount of flour on each big load he ground.

On the day that Jasper Quimble came, she saw the man take all the small bags of flour to his cart, then give Herbert some money for the bags.

What she didn't know was that this had been the share payment for the previous amount of flour.

Herbert didn't know that Sarah was watching him, and he went to the floorboard where he hid his hoarded money.

Setting aside the raised board, Herbert lifted out a sturdy box, opened it and put another small amount of coins into the box.

Locking it, he lowered it back down, and replaced the floorboard.

Sarah backed away and then making a little noise, came into the room.

Herbert looked pleased as she came into the room.

"Well Sarah dear, work has finished, and I am hungry. The question is, hungry for who?"

She squealed and ran over to him.

"You are a naughty man, and before dinner

too."

Herbert had a smile on his face as he returned to the living room and saw Sarah bustling around in the Kitchen making the meal.

"We have a nice lamb stew bubbling away here. I wonder my love if you would mind if I asked my father to join us. It's been a long time since he had a meal with us."

Herbert was in a happy mood. He had just enjoyed the fruits of being married to a vivacious woman and couldn't refuse her.

"Yes, my love, you run down and ask him to join us, I will stir the pot if it is needed."

Sarah pulled on a cloak and left Herbert.

A short while later, she returned and said, "Father will be with us in a short time." She then kissed her husband,

Herbert laid out the bowls and a knife, fork, and spoon.

As Sarah's father arrived, she said, "Just in time father, we are ready to dish up the stew."

Herbert pulled out a chair for his father-in-law, then sat down himself.

"Herbert dear," called Sarah, "Could you help me by carrying the pot with the stew?"

The willing husband rose from the chair and collected the pot and brought it to the table.

He watched his wife spoon out the stew, and soon they were enjoying the meal together.

It was after they sat down together that Herbert began to get a strange felling. His arms began to become weak and he seemed to have lost the ability to lift them or to move, the more he sat there next to Sarah, the more he became paralysed.

Sarah, who had been talking to her father, looked at Herbert then said, "I think he's ready now Dad."

They lifted Herbert out of the seat, dragged him across the floor to the hoist, then tied the ropes to his legs.

Sarah ran up the stairs to the top, pulled sacks of grain across to the hook. She looped the bags to the hook and pushed them over the gap.

They sank straight down, and Herbert went up.

Sarah now pulled Herbert from his upside-down position, onto the edge. She undid the tied rope from his legs then wrapped it around his one leg in a loop.

"Ready," shouted her father.

Sarah bent down to her husband and said to him, "Now Herbert, I am going away with my father, and we will be taking your nice big box of money with us. Unfortunately, you are not coming with us."

Herbert's eyes looked imploringly at her.

Sarah continued, "While you helped carry the pot of stew to the table, father poured a small amount of his potion that paralyses the limbs for a short while into your bowl. That's why dear husband, I must get on with what I must do. It has been fun, but now I need to become a widow, so it's time to say goodbye."

She bent and kissed him lightly on his lips and pushed him over the edge.

If Herbert had been able to scream, it would have woken the good people of Frampton

Cotterell, but alas, that had been taken from him.

Sarah's father saw Herbert crash to the floor and the rope drop down on top of him, followed by the sack of grain that also fell on him.

"Oh dear, what a shocking accident." Sarah's father said.

Sarah came back down, took the bowl and cutlery used by her father, and washed them up then dried and put them away.

Now no one would know that her father had been there.

Next, they lifted the floorboard and pulled out the large money box. This was taken outside and loaded onto the mills hand cart, and her father made his way to his house.

As soon as he was out of sight, she opened the big doors and started shouting.

People came from their homes to see what was going on and as they passed the new bride, who was crying and couldn't talk, they saw the body of the miller under the burst sack of grain.

She was consoled by the people and then the police came. Between her sobs, she explained that Herbert and she had had their meal then he had insisted he wanted to get the grain up into the top of the mill ready for the milling tomorrow.

It was as she was clearing the table, that Herbert had fallen down beside her followed by the grain sack.

Everyone commiserated with the poor woman, not long married. Never seen the miller so happy, all words said as the verdict of accidental death came in.

Sarah inherited the mill but explained that it had far too many memories to stay, so it was sold.

A few weeks later, after the sale, she returned to her father and stayed there for a short while.

Then someone remarked that the little cottage where they lived was now empty.

No one had seen them go, but the sign outside of the cottage said, 'For Rent'.

Sarah and her father were never seen again.

All that remained of the couple were the comments from the local people that for a brief while, Herbert had his taste of bliss.

Authors note

If you go to Frampton Cotterell you will find the remains of a Mill Tower dating back to the late 18th early 19th century. It is built of rubble stone and has a tapering, circular, four storey single tower.
There are four doors to the ground floor, three of which are blocked. It is said to be one of the best remaining windmills in the county.
Credit. Historic England

Cotterell is one of the names that migrated to our shores after the Norman Conquest. It is a name for a serf or bond tenant who held a cottage by service. The part 'Cote' (Old English) means shelter or cottage and 'rell' for realm.

Frampton is an Anglo-saxon name. 'Fram' is in part, taken from the river Frome. Frome meant fine or fair. The word 'Tun' meaning farm, added to this gave the name 'farm on the river.' (Framtun.)

Taken from the universal dictonary of word meanings. There are lot on line that give a like breakdown, but I thought you might like this one.

JP

Revenge is Sloe Sweet

Chapter one

It had been two years since Ezra and Sally had wed, but like an itch, Sally couldn't get the thought out of her mind that the Sheriff needed to have her revenge heaped upon him.

She never told her husband this, and her folly was never mentioned. But for her, it was still there.

Business in the forge was good and they had increased their turnover and thus their profits.

Sally helped with the working within the forge and when it was a day when the two men had to shut it down to clean it out, Sally and Emma went walking down the country paths to pick blackberries to make pies like blackberry and apple.

The men liked the result of their foraging and both ladies were happy with each other's company.

Emma was Ezra's mother, a buxom woman who never ceased to smile.

She had confided with Sally that she was pleased that she had joined her family, but that she was deeply sorry that it was through such tragic circumstances. She also mentioned that she hoped they would soon be grandparents.

Sally assured her that it was not for the want of trying, that her husband and she were not yet parents.

But that itch returned each time something like this was asked of her.

On this occasion, as they picked the fruit, they saw a monk picking berries and as they drew near, they greeted each other as people do.

"Good morning good people, I see that you are gathering Gods gifts that he so freely gives."

"Indeed, good Sir, we are gathering berries to make our husbands blackberry and apple pies," replied Emma, for it was seemlier for the elder of them to make a reply.

"Then we shall not quarrel over our bounty, for I am picking sloe berries to make wine for the brothers to drink as part of our sacrament."

Sally looked at the sloe's, big plump berries and decided to ask the monk a question.

"Would you tell me good monk; do you sell any of this wine to others outside of your group?"

"No mistress, what we make is for our use, we farm and provide for our needs."

"Thank you then brother monk, we must be on our way."

With exchanges of 'God go with you,' they parted.

As they returned up the path from the pool that the monks had settled near, Emma asked of Sally, "Why the interest in the wine they make?"

"I think it is the farmer in me," replied Sally, "for I have seen others picking such berries but not done so myself."

On the next market day, we shall buy a bottle of Sloe wine from the seller there, and we shall try this drink that has you so captivated."

Sally smiled at Emma, and said, "Thank you Emma, it will give my interest a chance to be satisfied."

They walked together and slowly made their way up to the rutted main road. They crossed the High street, so called because it was the peak of all the roads leading to it and returned to the Smithy.

Ezra came to her and kissed her, as did Emma to Edwin.

The men had finished clearing the clinker that always built up, and with the ash, had thrown this onto the roadway outside of the Smithy giving the wheels of the carts a better grip as they passed by.

The ladies passed through the forge to their living area behind it and then set about sorting out a meal for their family.

The meal was not much different from the meals she had made living with her father, but there was a change, for in this everlasting stew, there was always meat in it.

Emma looked in the stew pot and said, "I think we shall have more carrots in this, and potatoes. I will clean and chop up the offal we got from the butcher, and if you can add your herbs, this dinner will not take long."

They set to work, and it was not long before the cauldron was swung over the fire.

Then they set about making pastry for the pie. Sally peeled the apples as Emma made the pastry. Berries and apple were then put into another receptacle, and this was placed at the edge of the fire.

When the men returned from the ale house with their jug of beer, wonderful smells hit their nostrils.

The table was soon set up and once the ladies announced that all was ready, they all sat at the table.

Emma dished out onto the metal platters, and Sally passed each to the men then laid the others in their places.

The men had started their meal, as was always the case, and both women soon joined them.

Once the platters were cleared, the pie was cut, and with black juice running from it, each had a large slice.

It was after the meal was over, that Sally said she would need to forage for more herbs. Since she had become a member of the family and been adding her herbs to the cooking, they always adjusted the smithy work to leave her free to go and find them.

She had been thinking about the sloe's the monk had been picking.

Now she needed some information from a fellow farmer on the Claystairs farming that might be of use for her itch.

That night, she welcomed her husband's advances as she always did. He had been gentle with her, and she had grown to enjoy the union, but after, there was always that thought.

The following morning, Sally said goodbye to them all, and with a deep basket, she set out on her way.

She walked along the grass bank abutting the tracks made by the horse drawn carts and turned down a pathway that would bring her to the crossways. She crossed over the cross and continued down to Claystairs.

Once there, she looked for Gedon Fisher, for he could have an answer to her question.

As she worked her way along the hedgerow, she saw him in the distance, coming towards her.

Once they met, and the greetings were over, Sally got to the point.

"You have made sloe wine for a while now, haven't you Gedon?"

"Aye, that I have Sally. What's your interest in it then?"

"Could I try a little please?"

"Course you can, but mind thee, tis fearsome stuff."

"How so, Gedon?"

"Well lass, if you take in too much, it does give thee a belly ache."

"I would still like to try some please,"

"Come then Sally, for you know that I have it well hidden."

Sally followed Gedon down to the river Frome, then into the woods that was part of the Kings wood.

She had helped Gedon set up his distillery when he first started, now he had a large metal drum that he could put the pulp in and let it work its magic.

He ducked down and crawled through the brambles and Sally followed.

Gedon had cut into the side of the steep hill and mined inward to give himself a large area underground propped up with beams and supports. This was also where Gedon lived.

Infront of Sally as she stood back up, was the big drum that her husband had made for him.

"This is a young brew, but is still good to drink," said Gedon as he turned a tap to let some dark liquid pour out.

Sally looked at it, as he poured it into a cup.

It was a dark red colour and gave off a sour smell.

"There then Sally. This is it as it comes."

She looked at the third of a cup sample, then he took it from her.

"Now we mix the water and honey to sweeten and thin it down."

She watched as he put in another third of a cup of the mixture then moved it around with his finger to mix the two up together.

Sally again looked at the colour, slightly lighter now but no more appetising from the first stage she saw.

"Go on Sally, take a sip. Tis better than thou might think."

Sally lifted the cup to her lips, trying not to breath in the smell coming from the cup.

She took a small amount into her mouth and then moved it around before swallowing it.

It was better tasting than it looked.

"Why is it fizzy in my mouth?"

"Does happen always when I add the honey. The two don't seem to like each other."

" So, from the beginning, you boil water in

the tub. Do you squash the sloe's and remove the little seed?"

"No, I wash the dirt from them with a sieve, then squash them a bit and put them into this metal drum with the hot water. I do put some wild ginger roots in it. I clean them, then, hit the roots to bruise them. They go into the pot with the sloe's. I put the lid on it and cover the end with old cloth to stop the fly's. They like it an all."

"So, you only add the honey and more water after the sloe mixture has done its job."

"Yes Sally, Once I think it's done, I take a bucket of it out, put that thin cloth over the sieve, and pour it through into another bucket. I put the sloes that are out of the brew in a wheel barrel and it goes on the heap to rot."

He went on, "I swill the cloth in the river. I like to be clean doing this, then gets the next bucket. When the sieved wine is full up in the bucket, I pour it into the barrels over there and leave it."

"What would happen if you put it all into the big drum again and added the honey and water?"

"Don't know, never got enough to try. Folk do like it as it is, and I make a living."

"Right Gedon, you have a few barrels over there, I will buy one and if you can get it rolled along to Nightingale bridge, I will bring the horse and cart down to bring it back."

They settled on a price, and she left to pick a few herbs and then return to the forge to talk to Ezra.

The following day, she harnessed up the horse to the cart and drove along the High street to the old road, that took her to the hilly fields. This then led to the track that would take her to Frampton village, but over Nightingale bridge.

It was a warm day, and traffic was busy moving stock from the mill in Frampton to the bakery in Winterbourne. Others were carting goods from one place to another, and trading as they went.

Sally pulled up after crossing the bridge, then backed Goliath the horse and the cart into a big gap. She waited until a gap came, then pulled out, crossed the bridge, and pulled to the side.

Gedon was waiting for her.

She put a long plank of wood onto the back of the cart, and they both started to push the barrel up the plank to the carts body. It was tough work, but finally, it was done, they stood it up, put it at the head of the cart, and it was lashed into place.

Sally paid Gedon his money and reminded him that if what she wanted to do worked out, she would want more.

She left him as Goliath pulled the cart up the hill to the junction of the tracks in Yonder itself.

Sally guided Goliath to the left and followed the rutted track to the High street, she soon reached the next junction and turned left away from the Swan Inn who were changing horses for a Lords carriage. Which Lord, she knew not.

Making her way along the roadway, she reached the smithy and pulled up the horse and cart.

"Did you get it?" asked Ezra.

"I did, and not a drop was spilt. When will my tub be ready?"

"It's finished, but we will need to test it first. We have made the stand for it to rest on, and some steps to let you climb up to look inside."

Sally kissed her man, smiled, and said, "It will be worth it, I am sure."

Ezra untied the barrel and rolled it to the end of the cart. He jumped down, and then lifted it onto his shoulder, and carried it into the back room and through to the lean-to that served as a storage for metal and oddments.

He lowered the barrel and stood it to the side.

Everything was set now for Sally's next stage in the trial.

Chapter Two

It was four weeks before the froth on the top of the mixture died down.

Ezra kept saying that the Smithy smelt like a brewery, but nonetheless, he was keen to try Sally's concoction, and hoped that it would work.

She had been amazed how quickly the fermentation had started. Sally had put the boiled water that had been allowed to cool onto the wine, now in her tub. All four had had a sip, and said it was quite raw, and they would not be drinking that. After adding the honey, and some aromatic herbs, she covered it for two days then had a look. She left it alone after giving it another good stirring and hoped that the fermentation would soon cease.

Gedon said that his wine could be drunk after four months but improves with keeping longer.

If the men in the house had their way and it tasted good, it wouldn't keep.

Emma had been buying some full and half wooden barrels to put the wine in once it had been filtered.

Having waited for almost three weeks, Sally didn't want to wait much longer.

This time on checking the tub she saw the froth had now gone and a thin skin rested on top of the tub of liquid. It was time a taste test was due.

She climbed the ladder, reached in, and scooped out the skin from the top.

Whatever this was in the tub, the aromas now were something else.

Sally picked up the metal cup on a long handle that had been made for her and dipped it into the liquid.

Removing it she saw that she had a dark ruby coloured drink, but it was clear.

She unhooked a cup hanging from the side of the tub and poured it in.

Putting the long-handled cup down, she put the drink to her mouth and took a sip. It was slightly sweet and tasted absolutely wonderful.

Careful not to spill it, she went out to the workshop and stood still with a big grin on her face.

It was Edwin who noticed her first. He put down the tool he was holding and came around the forge.

"Is this what I think it is?"

"It is Edwin, and I bring thee a small sample for you to taste."

As he took the cup, he looked at it and said, "Look how clear it is."

He then took a sip, moved it around his mouth and then took another.

"Hey father, that's my share you've tasted as well as your own."

Emma came out to the forge and before Ezra could try it, she took it from her husband's hand and looked at it, then took a sip. Again, after moving it around her mouth, she took a larger mouthful.

"It's a wonderful elixir Sally," she said as Edwin took the cup from her and passed it to Ezra.

Ezra looked at the dregs in the cup, then said, "Oh well," and tipped it upside down to get the last dregs in the cup into his mouth.

He smiled at Sally, and said, "That little taster I got tells me you have done it my love."

"I think so my darling man, and now I want more to go into production.

"I will check it out once the job father and I are doing is finished."

"But you and I can try another small sample my dear," said Emma, smiling as she took the empty cup from Ezra.

Sally and Emma went into the lean-to, that now had sides to it, and was more a kind of shed.

Taking the cup from Emma, she went up the steps and again used the long-handled cup to get more of the wine.

They retreated into her mothers-in-law home and sat down, each having a mouthful from the cup then passing it on to the other.

"I can feel it heating me up, Sally, my goodness but it's good."

Sally was pleased with the elixir and needed to now strain the drink into the small barrels and get going on a much bigger batch.

A few hours later, the men dampened the fire down in the forge, and came in.

"Right," said Emma standing, then falling back into the chair. "Oh, my goodness, this elixir has taken me by surprise. I do believe that I might have been effected by the drink."

Edwin, Ezra, and Sally laughed.

They had their meal later after the men had been outside and washed themselves down.

Both the men had a cup of the wine, and Emma declined, having a slight headache.

There was a lot of talk about the new venture, and a few hours later, they separated and went to their own part of the home.

Sally welcomed Ezra into her arms and for the first time, she had no guilty feeling afterwards. Could her plan be having an effect?

The following morning when she went into the kitchen, all three were waiting for her.

"Sit down Sally, we want a word with thee," said Edwin.

Sally wondered what was going to happen,

had she done anything wrong?

She sat, looking at them.

"We have had a few words and we feel that thee should set up this elixir making in a space where you can make several barrels. How do you feel about doing the mixture again but in bigger amounts?"

"Well, it could be done, I said that I would like to get two barrels from Gedon next time. I know that the tub can take the two barrels full."

"No girl, we are talking about four or five tubs full next year. This is good wine elixir, and we think it will fetch a pretty price. What do you think Sally, could you do it if we set you up with a small barn that the tubs could stand in?"

"Oh, my goodness, I wasn't expecting that, but yes, if you could find a barn near here, and you could make the tubs and stands, then yes, next year I could do it. I would need help, but with a few friends to help and being paid by us, then it could be done. Can you find a barn near here?"

"We have a barn not too far from here near the bakery. We store all the oddments for the forge. If we built a lean-to and stored the usable metal in it, then the whole barn could be yours."

"Right then, you get your friend to sell you as much of his liquor as he can make, and you make your magic with that. When Ezra and I are not busy, we will make another tub for you and if you can get your magic ingredients for it all, you might make two full buts of the elixir wine before the end of the season," Edwin said.

The men went into the Smithy and started to revive the fire for the day's work.

Emma and Sally cleared the table from their breakfast, and Emma asked if she wanted an egg on toasted bread for her breakfast.

How things had changed for her since her, father's death. Now she could have egg's any time she wanted, and it wouldn't be a treat.

They toasted the bread over the fire in the forge on long handled metal fork.

Once she had finished her meal, she wrapped her thick woollen shawl around her, the wind was blowing from the north, and the first signs of autumn was showing.

She told Emma that she was going to try and find her friend Gedon to try and buy the two barrels of his wine.

Emma kissed her on her cheek and wished her gods speed.

Sally walked along the High street, then took the path across the common land to Crossways. She continued on as she had before, and ended up at the bottom of Claystairs, near the river.

She passed many of her farming friends that she knew when her parents worked the land. Finally, she saw Gedon.

Sally moved quicker and as he turned to walk up towards a turning into Yonder, she caught up with him.

"Hello Gedon, are you keeping well?" It was always better to get the small formalities out of the way.

"Ah, good to see thee Sally. You be looking in the best of health, I must say. Is all of thine well?

"We are all well Gedon."

"Hast thou come to tell me of thy failure on the barrel you paid me for, only you will need to see the Baron, he took most of it from me in his tax levy."

"No Gedon, but I do have some news for you. If you can supply me with as many barrels as you can, then I would like to buy them."

"Have you been doing this rebrewing thing you spoke about to me?"

"I have, and it works. Next year, in the sloe season, I want to take as many sloe barrels as possible of the wine you can supply me, or you can abandon your secret place and work with me next year. You could live in the barn; I am sure a home could be made in the rafters for you."

"Work for you?"

"Yes. You would clean the sloe's and make your wine as you do, but then it will come to me, and I will do my thing with it."

"And you will pay me for the season? I won't need to beg odd job work to tide us over."

"No Gedon. I couldn't have done this without you. You will be paid every week for every year you work with me."

"Every week. I can't take this in. And you want to buy all of my wine I have now?

"All of it Gedon."

"I warn you; I have four barrels standing and a half waiting for my next sale."

"Give me your price, and we can shake on it. I will bring the cart down tomorrow and meet you at Nightingale bridge."

They agreed a price, shook on it, and Gedon said he would round up a few people who would like to earn a halfpenny to roll the barrels to the bridge.

Sally returned and told them about the barrels, and how she had bought the lot.

They looked pleased then said, "We had a visitor today. The Lady of the Manor who had a wheel split on her carriage.

We had to wait for the wheelwright to cut two new spokes and fit it to the wheel, before we could fit the metal ring back on.

While she sat and waited, Emma offered her a glass of your elixir wine."

Everyone wanted to tell her about the visit and Sally found she was looking from one to another as the story was told in stages by them all.

"She didn't look very keen at first, but when Emma pulled out her absolute best wine glass, and poured the elixir, she seemed to change her mind," he continued.

"She remarked that it was a very noble wine, and if we had a barrel to sell, she would like to buy it," said Emma

"Emma told her that this was the first barrel from the tub, and we would only have two more at the most," added Edwin.

"She offered five shillings."

"Five," said Sally, thinking they have never received as much money in one go as this ever before.

"So, what did you say?"

"We said that you had made it, and we were

not sure if you wanted to sell it," said Ezra.

"She then said, Nonsense, I will pay you five shillings and six pence for the barrel and the same for another barrel if it's as good as this."

"We said yes, Sally. It wasn't ours to sell but as we are going to try to do this next year, we couldn't say no."

"It's fine, all of you own this as much as I do. We are a family, and it was a family decision."

They looked relieved and then said, "We still have the rest that is in the tub to strain and put in a barrel, that will help over the coming Winter months."

They all helped with the job.

Ezra and Emma drained the last of the elixir from the tub and filtered it through a muslin cloth. It stained it red, but Emma said she would wash it and then it could be used again."

"Oh, thank you all. Twas not a job I wanted to do on my own, but now that it is done, I can start a new batch. How much did it make, Emma?"

"There is one full barrel and one third in the other."

She was now ready for another batch.

Chapter Three

The following morning, she had a quick bite to eat, and as the men eased the forge back into life once again, she went out and brought Goliath to the cart. She backed him into place, then harnessed him up to the cart.

"You're going to earn your keep today my friend," she said as she rubbed his nose.

She pulled on her thick woollen shawl, and then said a silent word to God asking him not to let it rain, the cold was bad enough.

Once all was ready, she kissed her husband goodbye, and was soon on her way on the route to Nightingale bridge.

There was less carts or foot walkers on the route today, and she made good time to the bridge.

Once she had crossed it, she again backed Goliath and the cart into a gap, then crossed back over and pulled to the side.

She sat waiting, then Gedon came from under the bridge.

"I have the barrels Sally but thought I would keep out of sight of the nosey ones who come through here."

Sally got down from the seat and opened the carts back and then pulled the plank down to roll the barrels up.

Gedon waved two strong lads up to the cart and once they knew what to do, they went under the bridge and carried the barrels to the cart.

Repeating the job, they brought the next two full barrels to the cart.

One climbed onto the cart and rolled the barrel to the head of the cart and did the same for the rest. The other lad came with the half barrel.

This was moved to the head with the others.

Once they were all tied down, they jumped

down and Gedon paid them their money. She watched them walk up the hill away from Gedon and her.

"Have you given any thought to my offer Gedon?"

"I have Sally, and I would like to take thy offer up from next year. I have done well, thanks to you, my family will not go hungry over the Wintertime. I will come and see you in the New Year, and then we can make plans for the harvesting of that year."

"You will be welcome then. I will talk to Ezra and Edwin about the home for you all in the rafters of the barn once I return home."

"Then if I do not see thee before, Christmas tidings be upon thee and yours."

"And yours Gedon."

Sally clucked Goliath forward and he started up the hilly field track to the top, then again once in Yonder, turned on the left track and made her way slowly to the High street.

She again joined the carts going to Bristol and she made her way to Winterbourne, and the Smithy.

As she arrived, Ezra came out, and said. "Father and I are going to unload the barrels and take them through. Once tis unloaded, then you deal with Goliath and the cart."

Sally grinned at him and said, "Yes, master."

"At last she complies with her husband's wishes."

"Only this once husband dear," she said, and watched as he took a barrel from his father and carried it inside.

Once it was unloaded, she shepherded Goliath along. Then reversed the animal and the cart into the bay to the side.

She then walked the horse to the small paddock at the rear of their home.

As she came into the Smithy, she saw that a second tub was in the process of being made.

"We thought that as we were not very busy today, we would get started."

Sally told them about the talk with Gedon and they said they would get onto it.

Leaving the forge, she went into the place where the original tub was standing. It was on its side still empty, and Emma was almost inside the tub swilling it out and clearing all the bits from the bottom.

"Well Sally, I have just finished cleaning the tub, and the muslin cloth has been washed. It did stain it red, but we can use it again."

"Thank you, Emma. Shall we start the next lot?"

"And if you are agreeable, then I would take it kindly if you would let me help thee."

Sally smiled; they were all proud of her.

"Then we must start to boil the water and this time, we make twice as much as the first one."

They went into the forge and behind it, was a cauldron that could be filled and swung over the fires.

Both women filled buckets from the water container outside of the smithy, and humped the full buckets in.

They kept repeating this method until it was

full then asked if Ezra could pull it over the fire while they pushed with the rods they used when cooking.

It was a weight, but soon it was over the fire, and both women set to the bellows to increase the heat.

They left it to boil and sat on stools to talk over the future business of the clarification of the wine Gedon made.

Once the water was boiling, Ezra pushed and they pulled the cauldron from over the fire, and then left it to cool.

They sorted a meal for them all, strips of cold meat and cheese with chunks of bread.

The four relaxed for a short while but then a new request came for a pot repair, and the men went back to work.

Testing the water, they found it was warm, so started to bail out the water in buckets and take it through to the tub now up right and on the stand.

They had to climb the ladder numerous times while holding the bucket of water, and then pour it into the tub.

They became wet on the fronts of their long dresses with the spillage, but at last, the water was in it.

Ezra climbed the ladder and poured the barrel of Gedon's mixture into the wine and then did the same with the other. He then left them to get back to work.

Sally sorted out the herbs and doubled up on the honey. She heated this up over the fire, until it was very runny, then poured this in.

Her last thing was the aromatic herbs.

She gave it a stir and then put the lid on.

Tending the tub over the next three weeks and a bit was an anxious time, but now on looking inside the tub, the familiar skin was floating on top and no bubbles were rising from the mixture.

She skimmed the skin from the elixir and put it into a bucket; the pigs had enjoyed the last lot.

Next, she reached for the cup with the long handle and drew a sample out.

As she had done before, she poured it into a cup, looked at it, sniffed it and then took a drink.

It was slightly different in flavour, but still truly clear and felt hot to the throat as it slipped down.

She went into the Smithy and then as she entered, she stopped as she saw Ezra and Edwin with the Sheriff.

"Well, well. The woman herself. Good day to you Sally Bisp, I trust you are well."

The men watched her as she put the cup down, then moved closer to them.

"Good day Sheriff. What pray, has made you call to our humble home?"

"I was just explaining to your husband and his father here, that I had an occasion to dine with the Lord and Lady Codrington a few days ago. They told me that the good lady had to stop to have her carriage wheel repaired, new spokes and then the metal rim band heated back on. It seems that when she rested, one of you ladies, offered her a glass of elixir while she waited. She then shocked me by saying she had purchased a full barrel of the stuff and said she would have need for more."

"I was not here Sheriff, but what she told you was the truth."

"I never doubted her word, but it was the fact that you were making it, I could not believe."

"I did so under my husband's watchful eye Sheriff, and we both know how important a man is to a woman."

"Ah, Yes, indeed we do Sally. The point of my visit is to try the elixir myself. I cannot have those above me having knowledge that I have not been privy to, now can I?"

"So, you wish to try some of it, is that your wish Sheriff?"

"It is. Is that cup some of it?"

"This has not been tasted yet, I may need to put more herbs in it to give it a little more sweetness to the tongue. This is not ready yet, and we only have the Lady Codrington's order left."

"Then I will take her barrel, and once this new elixir is ready, you can sell her a barrel of the new stuff."

"I doubt that you would want to match her payment Sheriff, and for my husband to do that, you would need to do so."

"Do you suggest that I cannot pay for your barrel? You forget who you are speaking to."

"Forgive my rudeness Sheriff. I am aware of your importance."

"You will tell the Lady nothing, none of you. Now, fetch me the barrel and I will be on my way."

"And the money, Sheriff?" said Ezra, "What of that?"

"Tell me the amount she paid you and you shall have the same."

"She paid me five shillings and six pence for the barrel Sheriff," said Ezra.

"For a barrel of elixir that you have brewed between you. How do I know this was her price?"

"Our word, Sheriff. But you can ask her when next you dine with her."

"Very well, give me the barrel and I will send my servant tomorrow with the money."

"But Sheriff, the good Lady Codrington pays before she takes the elixir, and we know how a busy man like yourself can forget his promise the next day," said Ezra.

The Sheriff was seething. He looked at Ezra the Sally.

"Let me taste this elixir before I decide upon it."

"I will go and get a cup husband, if it be your wish," said Sally.

Ezra turned to Sally and said, "It is my wish Sally, for you to do so."

She went into the back room and poured a full cup from within the opened barrel.

Bringing the cup to Ezra, she passed it to him. And he passed it to the Sheriff.

The Sheriff sniffed it, then drank a small amount. He then tossed the remainder straight back and smacked his lips.

"It is indeed a goodly blend of elixir wine."

He then looked at Ezra and said, I will send the five shillings, but not the six pence. That is my tax upon the barrel. He then laughed.

He mounted his horse and rode on his way.

Ezra was angry, but Sally moved closer and said, calm husband, he is but a bully of a man."

She then turned, picked up the cup with the new elixir wine in it, and offered it to Ezra.

He drank a small amount, then grinned. "This one is slightly dryer to my tongue, but methinks it is a little better for it."

The cup was passed around and once empty, they agreed that although it was slightly different, it was as good as the first one.

As they sat eating their meal that evening, the Sheriff's man arrived and paid the five shillings for the barrel. True to his word, the six pence were not offered.

After the man had gone with the barrel, and the meal ended, they sat for a while before they went to their bedrooms to sleep.

Ezra made no move towards Sally but did hold her hand. She whispered to him that the Sheriff's visit had not upset her, and she would welcome him if he was of a mind.

"No Sally, tis the man himself who has made me in a turmoil. It is not thee my love."

She squeezed his hand and then turned away with her back to him. The Sheriff once again had caused pain in their life.

Chapter four

It took two days to strain the second elixir brew through the muslin cloth, and Emma had to buy two more sheets of it to finish the job, as wine was lost when the mesh clogged up.

At last they were able to count the barrels up and they were pleased to find that they had five full barrels and a half barrel that was full and another that was just over half filled.

It was on the following day towards the evening, that the Sheriff called on them again, demanding another barrel, less tax.

He dismounted and he smirked at Ezra and Sally as he said this.

"Sheriff, I think I must warn thee," said Sally, "If you imbibe vast amounts of this elixir wine, then you could suffer with the cramps, and I fear that thee might think ill of my husband and me."

The Sheriff turned to Ezra and said, "You should flog your woman more often, she has a rude tongue on her. No woman should open her mouth to tell a man how much he should drink."

The guards were laughing as they heard this said. One then got down from his horse and stood to the side of the Sheriff, as he looked at Ezra who was clearly angry.

"My wife spoke out of turn, but only out of care for you Sheriff. But I will say to you, the elixir has a strange way about it, and I would not wish you to suffer the ague that can be within the barrel through taking excess."

"I take my liquor like any other man. The volume does me no harm, other than weaken my legs as I go to my bed. Now man, bring me the barrel that I have come to pay thee for."

He opened a small money pouch and dropped the coins on the floor.

"Tell your woman to pick up your coins, for I will not place them in your or her hand."

Emma on hearing this, went to where the coins were and bent to pick them up.

Turning to Ezra the Sheriff pushed Emma to the floor and said, "I told you to tell your woman to pick up the coins, not for the other to do so."

Emma got up, her hands filthy with the mud outside the Smithy, and mud on her dress where she fell.

"My wife will pick up the coins when I tell her to, and it will not be now. You have shown dishonour to my mother, I will not let you do so to my wife again."

"Ah, so you do know. Very well, bring my barrel of elixir wine, and be done with it."

Edwin went into the back room and picked up a barrel and brought it out.

As he neared the entrance of the Smithy, the Sheriff said, "Stay just there. One of my men will come and take it from you."

He then leaned into the man by his side and said something quietly to him.

The man stepped forward with a grin, looked down at the five coins at his feet, and stepped on them pushing them further into the mud. He then walked up to Edwin and took the barrel.

Turning, he again stepped on the place where the coins were and pressed them further into the mud. The rest of the soldiers were laughing, and the Sheriff turned, nodded to them, and joined in with the merriment.

Sally was almost in tears, but clenching her hands together, she held on to her anger.

The barrel was strapped to a horse, and the Sheriff rode away with the lot of them laughing as they left.

Sally picked up a small shovel, and went to the place where the money had been trodden in.

Emma joined her, then both the men did also. Edwin was last to get on his knees and placed a bucket with water in it, so that as the coins were found they could clean them and themselves.

At last the five coins had been found and they washed their hands and dried them on the rags in the forge left for that purpose.

Over the evening meal, the four of them were quiet. Each running different thoughts of the encounter with the Sheriff.

The following morning, Sally said to them all that she wanted to go down the river and walk along it towards Damson bridge, where she picked the best herbs for her elixir.

She took her basket, but this time, she took a small hand spade. "If I find any wild garlic, then I shall get a few roots to use over Winter in our stews. It will help with the chills."

She went on her way and in an hour, was

walking along the bank looking for something she wanted.

At last she found the very thing, and taking her spade, she attacked the soil around it until the roots were exposed.

She cut a large piece from the plant and washed it in the stream.

Sally then turned and retraced her steps.

Once she arrived back, she told them all, she was going to do some work extracting some juice from her roots and left them.

Sally used a stone block to cut the root she had acquired and then she crushed it all.

She put it into a small metal bowl and went to the forge.

Taking a ladle, she poured a small amount of water into the bowl then placed it over the fire on a rack.

She watched and waited, and as she saw the bubbles coming from the root's, so the water disappeared.

Next, she removed the bowl from the fire, and took the root and bowl into the room she used for the making of the elixir.

Checking that no one was coming, she poured a large amount of the wine from a barrel into a large bowl and then put the cooked root into it.

She stirred it around and noted that the root was giving off bubbles as the wine soaked into the root.

Allowing the root to do its thing, she tested the result with her finger.

Slightly bitter.

She could adjust that.

Now was the time to put the wine and the roots magic, back into the barrel of wine.

Taking care, she poured the mixture back into the wine.

Placing the root bits on the block, she placed bricks and stones on it and watched the red juice come from the crushed root.

She guided the run of the juice into a cup, and when the juice finished flowing, she went to the wine and poured that in.

Sally pushed the wooden bung back in the barrel and rocked it back and forth.

Once she was satisfied it was mixed, she again opened the barrel and drew a small amount out.

The colour had changed and was not as clear as it was, but she still tried it.

It still had a bitter taste to it, but she could disguise this.

She took a small amount of honey and put it into a small metal bowl and placed it on the rack over the fire.

The men were working and took no heed of her.

Once it was like a runny liquid, she returned to the barrel, and poured it in.

Replacing the stopper, she shook it up again then let it settle before she opened it.

Again, she took a small amount from it, sniffed, and then drank a little.

Much better, the sweetness had done the trick.

She replaced the stopper and made sure that

it was in tight.

Next, she chalked on the outside, 'For her Ladyship.'

She then went into the kitchen and washed her hands in the warm water left to be reused.

Sally worked in the forge pumping the bellows as the men worked on a frame for a new carriage that a gentleman of business in Frampton had ordered. This would then go to someone else in Frampton to do the woodwork and the sewing of leather for the seats.

Two days later, again on an evening, the Sheriff called on them.

"I find the elixir wine very palatable, and to my taste. I want another barrel, and here's your coinage."

Again, he threw it to the ground, but this time as no rain had fallen, the coins lay where they fell.

Leaving the coins on the floor, Ezra started to walk into the back room.

Sally put her hand up on her husband's chest and said, "Don't take the one marked for her Ladyship, it is slightly sweeter, and blended to her requirements."

"What's that you say. Hold still Ezra, my man will go with you to see what's afoot."

Ezra waited until the soldier was with him, then went into the room with the barrels.

Both could clearly see the chalk marked barrel.

"Wait here, my master would like to see this."

He went to the Sheriff, who dismounted and

walked into the room.

He looked at the barrel, then said to Ezra, "I will take that one," pointing to the chalked barrel.

"But Sheriff, it is clearly marked for the Lady Codrington."

The Sheriff turned to Ezra and said, "Is she here, for I cannot see her?"

"No, but Sheriff."

"Has she paid you for this elixir wine?"

"No, but Sheriff, it is clearly made to her requirements."

"Then I shall enjoy it even more."

He turned to the man who was at his side, "Take the one marked with chalk, and that's an end to it."

The soldier lifted the barrel onto his shoulder and followed the Sheriff out to the forge and then to the horse that had no rider.

They tied the barrel onto it; the Sheriff and the soldier then mounted their horses.

"Give my compliments to the Lady when next she calls."

They then rode away.

Ezra turned to Sally and said, "When did the Lady Codrington order a barrel from us?"

She didn't husband, but she did say that our last lot of elixir was slightly more bitter, so I put a small amount of honey into that barrel for her."

Ezra nodded and turned and went to the doorway. Edwin had the coins in his hand and passed them to Ezra.

"Put them in our special safe place Ezra,

for there are rouges about, and will take any unguarded moment to relieve us of our money."

Ezra did as he was bid, and soon they were back to work.

Two days later, two soldiers rode up to the forge and said that the Sheriff was ill. Sally, Edwin, Ezra and Emma must go back with them. The Sheriff and his physician wanted to speak to them all.

Ezra went and got Goliath, while Edwin damped down the fire and closed the door.

The harness was soon on Goliath, and the cart was then hooked up.

They all mounted the cart, Sally at the back with Emma, who was looking very mystified.

Finally, they arrived at the turning to go down to the hamlet of Yonder, and the drove the horse and cart through the gate and stopped near the entrance to the Sheriffs home.

They were ushered into the bedroom and the Sheriff was laying on the bed, the foul smell of his being sick hit them at once. Not that any evidence was wanted, for the mess was on the floor.

As they stood there, the Sheriff clutched his stomach and spasmodic shudders caused him to void his bowl.

He was covered in leeches, and he was getting less and less able to move.

"Why are we here, has he got the plague?"

"He has accused you of poisoning him," said the doctor attending him, "but this is like nothing I have encountered before."

"Good Sir. My wife and I have warned the Sheriff that drinking the elixir wine in excess could have problems with his health. The Sheriff would have none of it and told me to thrash my wife for telling him how much he should drink. As to us poisoning him. He insisted that he took the barrel of wine that was being kept for the Lady Codrington. This was by his choice, and not in any way ours."

Ezra turned to the soldier in the room and said, "You were there and took the barrel from the room after he told you to do so. You didn't tamper with it to try and kill your master, did you?"

The man went white, "No, I did not, and it was as you say. The Sheriff told me to take the barrel with the chalk marks on it. I then tied it to the spare horse and carried it to his room where he drank most of the night."

"Show me," said the doctor, "and bring them also." He said pointing at Ezra and Sally.

They left the Sheriff who was now quiet, and went into a room with a large chair, and the barrel on a stand, with a mug beside it.

"Is it empty?" asked the physician.

The soldier lifted the barrel and shook it.

"A small amount is left in it."

"Pour the rest into a new tankard, not the one the Sheriff drank from."

The soldier poured the last little bit into the tankard, and the physician sniffed it. He passed it to Sally and said, "Drink this."

She took it and drank the wine.

"All of it."

She tipped up the tankard and finished the rest.

"I can see the chalk marks on the barrel, and your family would not have let you drink it if it had been poisoned.

He shook his head, then said, "I will check on the Sheriff, but I fear there is not a lot more I can do for him."

He went upstairs then returned, saying "The Sheriff has passed on. He has poisoned himself with excess alcohol, and it must be said, it was by his own choosing. Let these people return to their home."

The soldier showed them out, and they got onto the cart.

As they passed through the gate, Ezra said, "How strange that the Sheriff should die drinking wine saved for the Lady Codrington."

Sally smiled but said nothing as they returned home.

That was Sally's way.

Authors note

I have invented a name for the Lady of the Manor and used a local place name as a surname, hence Codrington.
I decided to write the second part to this story, because I truly felt it would be well received.
I know it's a longer story than you may have expected, but then, that's John's way!

Printed in Great Britain
by Amazon